SWEET RESTRAINT

THEIR BABYDOLL COLLECTION
BOOK 3

CALISTA JAYNE

Daddies' Sweetheart

Daddies Ever After

by Calista Jayne

ABOUT THE BOOK

Calling one man "daddy" is naughty enough—but two?

My creepy ex keeps popping up everywhere I turn.

My apartment is in shambles.

My life is spiraling out of control.

But a steamy encounter with not one but two commanding men shows me that maybe it's time to let someone else—or two someone elses—take care of me.

They have extreme expectations for what it means to be theirs...but after one taste of the pleasure they dole out, I'm hooked. I'll do anything, as long as they'll call me their babydoll.

This set includes the final two episodes of the Their Babydoll series.

Contents include: daddy kink, MFM sexytimes, spanking, BDSM, kidnapping by bad guys, violence and mental abuse by bad guys.

DADDIES' SWEETHEART

1

Ryder

I don't know what makes me do it, other than feeling some weird sense of something being not-right. I have no reason to talk to Jaxon right now. But as soon as there's a lull at Ironwood, I go into his office.

He looks up from his computer as soon as I step inside and asks, "Have you tried calling Olivia yet?"

She's on his mind, too, evidently.

"No," I say. "I was trying to give her space to chat with her mom."

Raking a hand through his dark hair, he says, "That chat is not going to go well. One of us should be home when Cal and Squid bring her back. She might be upset."

"I'll text them now and see if they have an ETA." I don't need to say it—I'm nervous as fuck. Something has my internal alarm making subtle beeping sounds. I can't be this freaked out over Olivia having a conversation about us with her mom, can I?

Pulling out my phone, I text Squid. *ETA for San Esteban?*

I wait a moment, but Squid doesn't respond to my text. Weird. I try Cal next.

"They're not responding," I say, and my internal alarm moves past its subtle beeping and starts blaring.

"Not responding?" Jaxon asks, going still. "Fuck. I'm sending Terrence and Cora up there."

Already, my fingers are flying over my phone and I dial both Cal and Squid. Maybe they couldn't text for some reason. But they aren't answering, either.

Spinning on my heel, I leave Jaxon's office. He's right behind me, barking orders into his phone.

We have Olivia's mom's address, because, well, we have every piece of info about Olivia at this point. I plug the street and number into my phone's navigation app and slide into the passenger seat of Jaxon's BMW.

Panic threatens to choke me. I won't let it. Right now, we have to be smooth and calm. I have to be strong for Olivia.

Whatever's happening, we'll fix it. She'll be safe. She has to be.

Another car is tearing out of the parking garage beneath Ironwood—that'll be Terrence and Cora, already on their way.

Jaxon jams the screen on the dashboard repeatedly, trying to call Cal and Squid. It's not going to work. Something has gone horribly wrong.

"We're an hour away," I say. "Call the police."

"On it."

I resume Jaxon's attempts to reach our guards while he deals with the dispatcher and drives us through clogged San Esteban highways. As soon as we get out of the city, it'll be faster going, but right now I'm ready to jump out of his car and run to Clear Springs, myself.

We're coming, Babydoll. We're on our way.

~

Olivia

The door is blocked. Smoke is filling the guest house—it's not a large building, maybe four-hundred square feet. Coughing, I pull up the neckline of my shirt so I can breathe through it like a makeshift filter. But my shirt can't keep the smoke from filling my throat. Nothing can.

I stumble to the nearest window and tug on the latch. Why isn't my mom coming to get me out of here? Where are Cal and Squid? Surely one of them has seen the smoke by now. Someone should be coming and they'll figure out how to get the door unbolted so I can get out.

The window is locked. I let go of my shirt to use both hands so I can wrestle with the rusted latch, but it's no use. It takes me a long moment to realize why—someone has affixed a padlock to it. I should've seen it right away, but my eyes are blurring with smoke-induced tears and the smoke is adding an extra haze to the mix.

Flames lick along the back wall, coming primarily from the bedroom.

The heat hits me in a wave, and I stumble. This fire isn't messing around.

Fine. A locked window. No big deal. I can break the glass. I am not going to die in this fucking guest house because I walked in like a too-stupid-to-live heroine in a crappy book, tricked by someone calling for help.

Looking around for something heavy, I turn toward the kitchen area. A frying pan ought to do the trick. After hurrying over, I yank open a cupboard. Several plastic bowls sit nestled in the front and I pull them out, cursing when there's nothing heavy behind them. I don't know where any shit is in this place. I go to the next cupboard. Perfect—it's full of pots and pans. Just as I'm reaching for a cast iron skillet, the window behind me smashes open.

I scream in surprise at the shattering glass, a high counterpoint to the dull roar of the fire.

An arm covered in a flannel sleeve knocks extra pieces of glass out of the way. "Come on!" a deep voice calls. "Are you in there?"

"Yes!" I shout, hurrying toward the window. The smoke is thick, obscuring my vision. I slam into the corner of the dining table. With all the adrenaline in my system, I barely register the pain as I limp to the window.

"Take my hand," the man says.

I don't ask questions; I just do as he says, and he pulls me through the window. I land in a heap in a rosebush, the thorns grasping my skin and tearing as I go down. But I'm out of the burning building, so I'm not about to complain.

My savior rushes away. His gait is familiar, as is his stature. It can't be...but it is. I know I'm not imagining him this time.

"Daniel?" I call.

He pauses, but he doesn't turn. Then he's racing off, out of sight.

Jaxon

Emergency vehicles surround the congresswoman's home —police cars, a fire truck, two ambulances. A couple of news vans, even. Shit.

Smoke rises up from behind the house. My heart jams itself into my fucking throat and remains there. There's immense pressure holding my body hostage, but I manage to park the car. Ryder and I get out without a word and jog to the front of the building.

Cal and Squid are being tended to by paramedics, but they're sitting upright on the front steps of the house. Olivia's mom is also being examined while sitting in an ambulance.

"Where's Olivia?" I demand.

Her mom points to the second ambulance, and my whole body goes cold. Olivia's lying on a stretcher, an oxygen mask covering her face. Ryder and I rush over there, pushing past a police officer. I don't hear anything, see anything, except her.

Ryder reaches her at the same time I do. The ambulance is full with Olivia and two EMTs, so we're stuck at the back door, looking in at her reclined form.

"Olivia?" Ryder says.

She sits up slightly, sees us. Through the clear mask on her face, I can see a weak smile. She gives us a thumbs up.

I can only stand there, staring while the EMTs treat her.

"Does she need to go to the hospital?" Ryder asks.

Olivia shakes her head, and one of the EMTs says, "No. Just a little oxygen. She inhaled some smoke, but not a critical amount."

I need to know what happened. She inhaled smoke? There must have been a fire—that cloud of smoke I saw in the sky as we drove up. Shit. I can't handle this. How did it all happen?

"Excuse me," a voice says from behind me.

I turn around to face the police officer we brushed past. "Yes?"

"I need to know who you are and what your business is. This is a crime scene and you shouldn't be here at all."

"I'm her boyfriend," I say.

The officer gives Ryder a pointed look. "And...you are?"

Olivia's voice comes from behind us. "He's my other boyfriend."

To his credit, the officer doesn't miss a beat. "May I ask what you both are doing here?"

"We're also in charge of Olivia's private security," I say.

"Those two bodyguards on the steps over there are from our company," Ryder adds, pointing to Cal and Squid. He pulls a business card from his wallet and hands it to the officer.

A smoke detector blares from inside the house. Several fire fighters rush into the building.

Olivia's mom is out of her ambulance and standing, although she supports herself on the edge of the vehicle. "That's probably my quiche," she says miserably. "I don't know why everything went wrong today."

I have a suspicion, and that suspicion is Olivia's ex-boyfriend, Daniel.

Turns out, it was the quiche burning, and the fire fighters get that sorted and return to the driveway, where they're presumably waiting for the rest of their team.

It takes far too long to disentangle ourselves from all of the emergency personnel and services. Ryder makes sure Cal and Squid are taken care of. Cora and Terrence are in charge of driving them back to San Esteban. Cal and Squid were each shot with a tranquilizer dart, as was Olivia's mom, which knocked all three of them out while the arsonist led Olivia to the guest house, locked her in, and started the fire.

Olivia gets the go-ahead to come home with Ryder and me. I drive, and Ryder sits in the back with her. We don't speak, although I have so many fucking questions, I could explode. But Olivia's exhausted. Ryder has her right up against him, and she rests her head on his shoulder. Her eyes meet mine from time to time in the rearview mirror. I wonder if she remembers that night, not too long ago, when we rode like this to Ryder's cabin, only it was him driving, and me sitting in the backseat with her.

Once we're back in the penthouse, Ryder carries Olivia right over to the sofa and sits with her cradled in his arms. She reaches for me, so I sit next to them and pull her feet into my lap. I take off her shoes and absently rub her feet—my attention is on her emotions and what she's gone through today.

"Don't try to sugarcoat it," I tell her. "How are you feeling?"

Scrunching her nose in thought, she says, "I'm okay. Not great, but okay. It was scary, but I got out."

My chest clenches at the rough sound of her voice. All that smoke. God, it could have been so much worse.

"You got out through a broken window," Ryder says, looking over the many cuts on her arms. The cuts are superficial, thank fuck. Ryder continues, "Is that what sliced you up?"

"No, he dragged me out and I landed in a rosebush."

"*He*?" Ryder asks. "I assumed you got out on your own."

She sighs. "So this is going to sound weird, but some guy showed up. He broke the window for me while I was looking for something to use. Then he helped me get through it."

There's more than what she's saying. My hands go still where they were rubbing her feet. "Some guy?" I ask.

Her gray eyes are serious as she says, "I think it was Daniel."

"The fuck?!" Ryder exclaims.

Olivia winces. "I know, I know it's crazy. I was afraid to tell you because I know you'll think I'm nuts."

"We don't think you're crazy, Babydoll," I say. "I don't know about Ryder, but I'm pissed as hell that Daniel put this whole thing together."

"Well," she says, "we don't know that Daniel's behind it. After all, he saved me."

Ryder's scowl is pronounced as he looks at Olivia. "Not sure it counts as 'saving' when he set up that whole situation to begin with."

"Did he, though?" Olivia asks.

There's a long moment when all three of us seem to be weighing that idea. Then Ryder says, "Well, who else?"

Genevieve is gone. She faced charges for what she did at Olivia's gala, but they aren't serious, and whatever legal shit she has to work out, she's doing it from somewhere else.

"It just seems strange he would go to all that trouble," Olivia says. "Knocking out my mom, Cal, and Squid— only to set the guest house on fire and trap me in there... and then set me free."

"Who knows how his sick mind works?" Ryder asks. "Maybe he just wanted to scare you."

"Maybe," Olivia says. "But there are other ways to scare me that don't take quite so much effort."

She has a point, but so does Ryder—who knows how Daniel's sick mind works?

She seems disappointed by our skepticism. "You don't believe me."

"No, we believe you a hundred percent. You saw Daniel, and he helped you get out," I say. "Neither of us thinks you're crazy. We're just trying to wrap our heads around the whole thing, same as you. Besides which, how did he know where you were? Whether to set this up, or to save you?"

"I don't know." She sighs and leans her head against Ryder's shoulder, inhaling deeply. "You smell good, Mr. Ryder. I don't want to think about today anymore."

"Really," he says. "How do you suggest we take your mind off of it?"

Squirming in his lap, she grins widely. "I think I found just the thing to take my mind off of it."

Ryder chuckles and gives her a brief kiss on the lips. "Something about escaping life-threatening danger seems to make you horny."

"Everything makes me horny." She sticks out her tongue at him.

"Are you trying to be a brat," he asks in a stern voice, "or does it just come naturally to you?"

"Daddy," she says, "Ryder's being mean to me again."

"Nope," I say, letting go of her legs. "I need to check in with work, make sure everyone's ready to ramp up security."

"Again?" Olivia asks.

"Yeah. I'll sit right over here, though, and if Ryder wants help punishing you for your sassy mouth, I'll be ready."

Ryder's already snaking his hand into Olivia's hair and grabbing it into a ponytail so he can direct her head. "You stuck out your tongue at me, little girl. I have a much better use for that mouth. On your knees, *princess*."

2

Jaxon

Olivia moves awkwardly because Ryder's still controlling her head with the makeshift ponytail, but she manages to slide down off of his legs and kneel between them. One-handed, Ryder unbuckles his belt and unfastens his pants.

I move to the other sofa and pull out my phone, one eye on Olivia, who's licking her lips as she looks at Ryder's lap, and one eye on the messages coming in from work. I fire off a missive to our HR department, telling them we need to hire more guards. Ironwood isn't big enough to protect Olivia and all of our existing clients. And even if Olivia didn't need our help, it's time to expand. That's what I met with our investors about.

Ryder directs Olivia over his cock, pulling her back when she gets too enthusiastic, tapping the head on her lips to tease her.

"Mr. Ryder, please," she says. "I love having you in my mouth."

His face flashes with disapproval before he schools his features. Something's bothering him, but he doesn't want her to know. Or maybe he doesn't want me to know. Shrugging, I return to my email and try to focus despite my cock hardening in my pants.

Ryder allows her to suck him, and she bobs up and down on his cock. She moans in pleasure, then makes a sound of disappointment when Ryder forces her away.

"Stand up," he says, his voice rough.

From the corner of my eye, I watch as she does as he asks, standing before him in the respectable-looking blouse and skirt she wore to her mother's house.

"Undress," he says.

I wish I could capture this on film, but no lighting would properly allow Olivia's perfect blush to come through. She slowly unbuttons her blouse. Ryder's gaze is intent on her chest, on her moving fingers. Once the shirt is unbuttoned, she shrugs it off, sets it on the coffee table behind her, and stands before him in her skirt and a lacy white bra.

Remembering that I'm supposed to be working, I return to my email. When I look up again, Olivia's down to her panties, lacy white to match the bra she is no longer wearing, and Ryder has stood up. He circles her, touching her lightly on her shoulder, waist, hip. He palms the globes of her ass and gives her a light swat, which causes her to gasp.

A large bruise has blossomed on the side of her thigh. Neither of us have put it there; we don't leave lasting marks, and that kind of bruise doesn't look like it would've been fun in any way.

"What's this?" Ryder asks, pointing at the bruise.

"Ran into a table," she says, "when I was leaving the guest house."

Bending forward, he presses a soft kiss to the mark.

"Thank you, Sir," Olivia says, giving him a smile full of affection.

"You're welcome," he says in a gruff voice.

He trails a hand along the lower edge of her panties, then inside. Pulling his hand away, he lifts it up to his mouth and sucks on his finger. "Fuck, that's good. Give Jaxon a taste."

Olivia puts her hand into her panties, then brings it out again, two of her fingers glistening with her arousal. "Daddy? Do you want a taste?"

I grin at her. "Always, Babydoll."

She takes the few steps over to stand in front of me and holds out her fingers. I allow her to slide them past my lips, then I swirl my tongue over her wetness. So sweet. I still have a few messages to tend to, but at this point, I'm not sure whether I'll get to them before or after I fuck Olivia.

Still, the freak in me loves watching her and Ryder together, so after I've licked her fingers clean, I pat her thigh and say, "Back to Ryder, little one," and I try to pay attention to my phone once more.

Ryder whispers something in her ear, and she gives him a frown, shakes her head.

"Now, Babydoll," he says.

Looking uncertain, she leaves the room.

I raise my eyebrows at Ryder. "Where'd you send her?"

"Nipple clamps." His smile is full of sadistic delight.

"Awesome. I haven't played with those with her before."

"Are you almost done with the work shit?" he asks.

"Nearly. Don't hold back on my account, though."

Olivia returns to the living room. She's holding the clamps, which are joined by a chain. Ryder takes them from her and goes to the kitchen, where I hear water running. They aren't new, so he's sterilizing them with soap and hot water even though we always wash toys right after using them.

Olivia shifts from foot to foot, looking nervously around the room.

"Doing okay, sweetheart?" I ask.

"He's going to hurt me," she whispers.

I want to laugh. "And you're going to love it."

I wonder if she'll bolt like she did that time when I threatened her with my belt at the cabin. That was fucking fun.

But if she was considering it, she gives up when Ryder returns to the room, his hand closed over the clamps.

Olivia covers her tits with her hands.

"No, wait," she says.

Ryder grins. "*No, wait* isn't your—"

"Isn't my safe word, I know." She rolls her eyes.

"Ooh, you're such a brat," he says, grinning wider. "I love punishing brats. Show me your tits, little girl. I have some special jewelry for them."

"Mr. Ryder..."

He waits, listening for a real argument, but she doesn't have one. She purses her lips together.

"Oh, princess," he says, cupping her cheek. He leans down and kisses her mouth, wrapping an arm around her back while taking his other hand and pushing the chain against one of her nipples, scraping her with it gently.

Her eyes fly open in alarm, but he continues kissing and scraping, and after a moment during which I am definitely *not* paying attention to my email like I'd planned, she relaxes in his embrace and gives herself to the kiss.

It's so hot how she loses track of everything else when we kiss her. Like every thought just flies out of her head and she's a slave to lust.

Ryder eventually ends the kiss, but he keeps the chain of the nipple clamps against Olivia's chest.

"Good girl," he whispers. "Are you ready to take this for me?"

Eyes wide, Olivia nods and bites her lip.

He fiddles with one of the clamps before fastening it to one of her nipples. She sucks in her breath.

"Ow, ow, ow." She tries to bat his hand away.

"Let me do this," he says. "You can take it, and I promise you, you're going to like it. Have either of us ever been wrong about something like this?"

She shakes her head. "You've always been right."

"That's right," he says, kissing her again. This time, during the kiss, he puts the second clamp on her. "Does it hurt too much?"

Her lips are parted, swollen from his kiss, and her

chest moves with every breath, causing the chain and clasps to catch the light filtering in through the windows.

"You look so pretty like that," Ryder says. "Doesn't she, Jax?"

I set down my phone. There's no fucking way I'll be able to concentrate now, not with Olivia looking like that, and half-mad with need. She moves her legs slightly, as if seeking friction, relief for her unused pussy. "She looks very pretty," I say.

"Pretty enough to share with the world, I think," Ryder says, as if an idea has just occurred to him. "Walk over by the windows, Babydoll."

"What? Someone will see..."

They won't, because the glass doesn't work that way. I wonder if Ryder will keep that a secret, like I would, but he says, "One-way glass. We can see out, no one can see in. Now get that gorgeous ass over there before I have to tell you twice."

Clad in only her panties, she scampers to the window but doesn't walk all the way up to it. Hesitating a few feet away, she says, "I feel like anyone could just look in here and see me."

There are two more high-rises across the avenue running along this side of the building. If I didn't have the windows made of this glass, yeah, it would be entirely possible for people across the way to see in. Some of those are offices, and we would be able to see people sitting at their desks and working, if we were to really stare.

"Against the glass, Olivia." Ryder's voice is even and low.

She inches closer, but she's still about two feet from the glass.

Ryder marches over to her and forcibly moves her until her tits, still in the nipple clamps, press up against the window. He nudges her feet apart with his foot, spreading her legs, then removes her panties, baring her. Next, he arranges her hands on the glass.

"This is what I meant," he says, his voice almost too low for me to hear.

Goosebumps spread over Olivia's skin.

"Arch your back for me, baby," Ryder says. "Bring your legs back a couple of inches. I want your tits on the glass, your ass back here toward me."

She complies, despite the awkward position.

Ryder strokes a hand over the curve of her back. "Well done."

His hand travels lower, over her ass, and he stops between her legs. Olivia moans while he plays with her. I have to reach down to my cock and squeeze it because the scene is just that fucking amazing.

When Ryder takes his hand away from her pussy, Olivia moans in protest. But he's only taking off his shirt and unbuttoning his pants, shoving them down just low enough to free his cock. He pushes Olivia's legs farther apart and guides himself past her entrance. Olivia arches her back, which presses her tits harder against the window.

"Yes, sweetheart," he croons, pushing all the way into her. "Hold on, so you don't bang your face against the glass. Jaxon's watching you. Do you think maybe, just maybe, the glass isn't one way after all, and all those other people in their offices and apartments can watch you, too?"

She shakes her head like the idea is distasteful, but the flush that creeps over her skin and the little moans she makes tell a different story.

"Jaxon keeps squeezing his dick," Ryder says, all while thrusting in and out of her, his hips slamming against her ass with each in-stroke. "I bet some of those accountants across the way are getting off to this, too—the sight of your pretty tits in that jewelry, your legs spread, and my cock filling your cunt."

He brings a hand around to her neck and her eyes flutter shut in delight as he applies pressure.

"Mr. Ryder," she cries, her body seizing as an orgasm takes her.

"Fuck, Babydoll, your pussy feels so good squeezing me like that. Yes. Fuck." Ryder tenses up with his own orgasm. He bows over Olivia's back, breathing hard.

I know exactly what Olivia's pussy feels like with its rhythmic pulses during her orgasms, and my damned dick is leaking at the idea of being buried in her in the same way.

Ryder whispers in Olivia's ear, and she turns to look over her shoulder at me. He says something again, and she nods. He grabs the chain dangling between her nipple clamps and leads her to me. It's a delicate balance of how close she has to stay to him to avoid a sharp tug, and her face twists in pain and pleasure with nearly every step.

"Fuck, you're gorgeous," I say.

"Can I sit on your cock, Daddy?" she whispers.

"It's been waiting just for you."

"I'm going to be messy." She bites her lip. Her cheeks, neck, and chest are still flushed.

"I fucking *love* messy," I say. Cream-pie porn doesn't do it for me, but the thought of Olivia climbing into my lap, already dripping with sex, definitely does it for me. I unfasten my pants and shove them down to my thighs.

Her legs are shaking from her first orgasm and her position against the windows, so Ryder helps her climb onto my lap. I give the chain between her breasts a gentle pull, and she gasps. Holding up my cock, I let her lower herself onto me.

Wet, messy. She's tight and swollen from her orgasm, but I glide right in. I fucking love it.

"Our sloppy little Babydoll," I whisper, cupping her cheek. "I love you. You're amazing. Are you ready to ride Daddy?"

She nods. "But my legs are tired. I don't know how long I can go."

"We'll take care of you, sweetheart," Ryder says, his voice affectionate.

The man's come so far from where he used to be with Olivia—closed-off, acting like nothing affected him. Now a bruise can cause him to stop what he's doing and kiss it better. I cup my hand over the same bruise and look into Olivia's eyes. "I hate that you got hurt. I hate that we weren't there."

Her gray eyes fill with tears. "I know, Daddy. I'm sorry."

"It's not your fault, Babydoll."

I run my fingers around the clamps, appreciating the way they emphasize her nipples and pull the skin. "How is it feeling?"

"Bad," she says, "and good."

Reaching to where we join, I slide my fingers over her clit. She shudders and begins to rock, her hips moving back and forth, up and down my cock. The friction, her heat, the glide of her arousal mixed with Ryder's come—it's fucking exquisite.

Ryder stands to the side, watching in approval. His dick is already half-hard again, and I wonder whether he's going to join in, but for now he seems content to just watch. Which is fine, because Olivia's energy is flagging.

I sit forward and lift her. She gives a moan when her nipples brush against my chest in their clamps.

"Let's get those off of you, sweetheart," I murmur, and Ryder reaches in to help me so I don't have to set her down yet.

She hisses out a breath when each nipple is freed. They look swollen, sensitive, so I lean forward and pull one into my mouth. Her hips twitch and she presses her pussy all the way down on my cock, as much as she can take, griding her clit against my pelvis.

"Just a minute, little one," I say, carrying her to the bedroom. Once there, I lay her on her stomach on the bed and climb behind her.

I nudge her legs apart with mine and slide into her pussy. "Do the sheets feel good on your poor, abused nipples?" I ask her.

"Mmmf, *no*," she says.

"Excellent," I say, and Ryder chuckles. "Hang on tight, sweetheart. This is going to be rough."

She grips the sheets and I start fucking her, hard and fast. Her moans rise in volume. Ryder reaches for his dick and jacks himself off while he watches. My body tenses with each thrust, preparing itself for an orgasm. Olivia's pussy tightens where it grips me, and she arches her back, trying to meet my thrusts despite being pinned down.

"Watch Ryder," I tell her. "Eyes on him."

She turns her head to the side so she can see him.

Our orgasms are imminent, my body fire where it meets hers. Every movement is beyond my control—it's all just about fucking, reclaiming our princess, making her ours again, reassuring my heart that she's safe, that she belongs to us.

"I'll never let anything bad happen to you," I grunt as my thrusts grow more frenzied.

"Daddy—I'm so close," she says.

"I got you," I say, and reach beneath her to rub her clit. There's no finesse to my movement because of the position, but it seems to do the job and she screams with pleasure, throwing her head back.

Ryder orgasms, and thick spurts of his come coat Olivia's shoulders and upper back. I'm there, too, pumping into her, emptying everything.

It's all for her. All of me, everything I have.

And it always will be. Even if she doesn't believe that yet, it's the truth, and I'll spend the rest of my life convincing her if that's what it takes.

3

_____

Olivia

Jaxon and Ryder get wet, warm washcloths and gently run them over my back, clearing off the evidence of Ryder's release.

"I kind of regret washing you off," Ryder says. "I like the idea of you wearing me all night, you filthy princess."

"I wouldn't mind," I say, turning my head and blinking up at him. I remain stomach-down on the bed, my body limp. I'm so sleepy. It's only early evening, but this day was a long one.

"Maybe another time," he says, bending to kiss my lips.

I prolong the kiss, even though I know he meant it to be a quick one, because his lips are perfect and he tastes divine—all forest and wilderness.

He sighs when he finally pulls away. "I love you, Olivia."

"I love you, too."

He smiles, then opens his mouth, then closes it.

"What is it?" I ask.

"I hate to go," he says, "but Jax set some things in motion at the office, and we should probably keep them moving..."

"I can stay here for a bit," Jaxon says.

I turn over so I can frown at him. "I don't need a babysitter."

His warm brown eyes are kind, yet stern. "You were just attacked and you barely escaped a burning building. Maybe *you* don't need a babysitter, but *I* need one of us to be with you. Ryder can work right now, and I'll go in later, when he's home."

I'm not loving the idea of being babied, but he has a point. Can I let them pamper me...not for my sake, but for theirs? I guess there are worse things in the world than having two boyfriends who want to take care of me.

My eyes fill with tears. I'm so fucking lucky. I'm lucky to have them. I'm lucky to be alive.

Ryder kisses me goodbye. "I'll be back tonight, Babydoll."

"See you soon, Mr. Ryder." I wink at him.

He smiles, but it's forced. He must be stressed about today and all the work that needs to happen. I wish I didn't need protection. I wish everything was safe.

The swoosh of the elevator doors opening and closing seem unnaturally loud in the new quiet as Ryder leaves.

"Hey, sweetheart, what's wrong?" Jaxon asks, climbing into bed to lie next to me.

"Maybe we should go somewhere," I say.

"Go somewhere?" Jaxon runs a hand along my bare arm. "Where do you have in mind?"

"Maybe...somewhere far away."

"Hmm," he says. "Is this a vacation or an escape?"

"Both?" I sigh. "More an escape."

Maybe something, too, to keep me away from my mother. If I hadn't escaped in time and found my phone at the gazebo, I wouldn't have been able to call the fire department. My mom's back yard is full of trees. It wouldn't have taken much of a breeze for the fire at the guest house to connect to the main house, where she'd been lying on the floor, unconscious.

A tranquilizer dart. I hadn't seen it at first and my panic at seeing my strong, capable mother lying on the kitchen floor, her blond hair splashed against the tile? Even the memory of it is making my chest feel tight and panicky.

"Olivia, baby, breathe," Jaxon murmurs, stroking my hair, bringing me back to the here and now.

I burrow my face against his chest, inhaling the faint citrus scent that clings to him. There, held fast in his protective arms, I let the terrors of the day fade away, and I sleep.

Ryder

The day after the fire, I check my phone when I wake. The media is well on its way to buzzing with conspiracy theories about who set the congresswoman's house on fire, and why. I'd seen a couple of news vans parked outside the home, but I'd ignored them as best I could. Irritatingly, they got a video clip of Olivia being escorted into the back of an ambulance, which pisses me right the hell off. She never asked for that kind of attention, and it's the sort of image that dickheads like her ex would get off to.

Jax and I slept on either side of Olivia last night. She was restless, flipping over numerous times before landing in my arms, and then Jaxon's, and back again.

She wakes up and comes into the kitchen and dining area soon after I do, with dark circles under her eyes. She accepts the smoothie Jaxon blends for her, then slumps into the living room with her phone.

"Our little girl is a zombie today," Jaxon remarks.

I nod. "I can work from here today, keep her company."

"Thanks." He says goodbye to Olivia and goes into the office, so I settle myself at the dining room table.

Every few minutes, a soft *ping* comes from the living room, where Olivia's sitting with her phone. Otherwise, it's deathly quiet in there. I get up to investigate, and find Olivia sitting on the couch with her arms wrapped around her knees, holding her phone, and crying.

"Baby," I say, rushing forward. "What's going on?"

"They're saying I'm—that I'm—I'm responsible for the fire," she says.

"What the fuck?" I hadn't seen that particular theory. Gently prying the phone from her hands, I look at the text Samantha has just sent her. The headline reads *Unhinged Daughter Source of Congresswoman's Fire?* "Oh, fuck this, sweetheart. They don't know what they're talking about."

"How can they say these things?" she asks, looking up at me. Her eyelashes are wet with tears, and her cheeks are wet as well.

With my free hand, I wipe away her tears as best I can. "Because they're dumbasses, all of them. Why is Samantha sending this shit to you?"

"She thought I should know..."

"She's wrong. I mean, you should know. Just not like this, and not right now."

Giving a shuddering breath, Olivia says, "She's just trying to help."

"I'm not saying she's a bad friend," I say, setting Olivia's phone on the coffee table and sitting next to her. I lift her onto my lap, the way we sat yesterday after coming home. Damn, she feels so good in my arms, warm and cuddly, her lush ass warm against my dick. I breathe in, my cheek pressed to her hair. "I have to get some work done, but I'm just in the other room. Can I put a movie on for you, so you can zone out for a little while?"

"I guess. I should work, too. There's so much to get done for Youth Arts—"

"It'll wait. You could use a day off where you're not checking texts or social media, or the news. I think that's best. Do you agree?"

She sighs. "I guess so."

Brushing a quick kiss against the top of her head, I say, "Great. What do you want to watch? Car chase? Superheroes?"

Her mouth purses while she thinks. "Maybe a spy thriller. James Bond."

"On it." I set up a movie for her and bring her a blanket. "Call for me if you need anything, even company, okay? I'm working, but I can take breaks as often as you need me."

"I always need you," she says with a saucy wink.

This girl. She's fucking wonderful. Sweet, sassy. Perfect for me.

As the opening song blares on the Bond flick, I start toward the dining room. Then I spot Olivia's phone on the coffee table.

"I'm confiscating this," I tell her, snatching the device.

She shrugs, her eyes glued to the television. "Text Samantha back for me, if she texts again? Let her know I'm taking a break."

"Will do, sweetheart."

Back in the dining room, I settle into my review of potential new hires. HR has screened them, of course, so now it's up to Jaxon and me to see who might be the best fit. I'm tempted to hire them all, because we need the extra guards.

I review the notes from Jax's meeting with the investors, as well. It's looking good. Expansion will suit Ironwood, even though we don't need the money or anything like that. As long as we don't have to work any harder, I'm all for it.

Olivia's phone buzzes with a text from Samantha.

"What's your passcode, Olivia?" I call.

"Five-five-six-six," she says.

I tap it in and respond to Samantha's text. *Hi, Samantha. This is Ryder. Olivia's taking a break from her phone and from the news.*

Got it, she texts back. *Tell her to call me if she wants to talk.*

Will do.

I relay Samantha's message and then get back to work, but no sooner do I start my deep-dive into one applicant's social media presence, than a new message pops up on Olivia's phone, this one from an unknown number. The preview is right there at the top of her screen.

You should be more careful, Olivia.

Sounds fucking ominous. What kind of friend would send her *that* kind of message? No friend at all, I'm guessing, if it's an unknown number. And it shows me that there's an attachment. Irritated, I tap in Olivia's passcode again so I can see more.

The attachment is a video.

I don't click on it right away. Maybe I should ask Olivia before opening it, but I'm betting no good will come of this. Still, I peek at her in the living room. Well, that answers that—she's fast asleep while Bond-James-Bond works hard at stopping another supervillain from fucking up the world.

Going back to the dining room, I click on the attachment. It takes me a moment to register what I'm seeing. Everything is dim and grainy. There's something in the background—tall, like the forms of two people standing, wrapped up in one another. The way the shadows fall makes it seem like there are actually three forms instead of two.

It's Olivia's sculpture. I recognize it, now, from photographs.

The camera approaches the sculpture. A hand holding a crowbar appears in the bottom of the frame.

Holy fuck. I don't want to watch this.

But I allow the video to keep playing, because I need

to see it all. I've seen it already, in fact, from the security cameras Jaxon and I had set up in Olivia's studio early on. The man—Daniel, I know, from the security footage, hits the sculpture with the crowbar. Ceramic breaks, shatters. He hits it again and again, smashing the artwork into bits.

Every hit physically pains me, because I know it means pain for Olivia.

There are other sculptures in the studio. I force myself to watch him break apart each one. The sound is awful, and I lower the volume so it won't wake Olivia. Ceramic shards litter the floor, and the stands where the sculptures stood are now covered in dust and jagged pieces.

When he's done, he tosses the crowbar up in the air before catching it, like he's pleased with a job fucking well done. Then the video goes blank. It's over.

The text that accompanied the video—it wasn't a warning, it was a threat.

You should be more careful, Olivia.

I can't let her see this.

I don't even want to tell her about this. She's strong— one of the strongest people I know—but she's been through so much the past month.

Whether or not I tell her, I can't pretend there was no message. This kind of shit is serious.

I dial Leonie at Ironwood. After I recite my security code, she says, "What can I do for you?"

"I got a text, with a video attachment. Is there any way to trace the phone number, IP address, or any of that other technology shit?"

"Technology shit, that's a technical term," she says in a wry voice.

"Yeah, come on. What can you do with it?"

"Forward it to me, and I'll try."

I hesitate.

"Ryder?" she prompts.

"It's coming from Olivia's phone. It wasn't texted to me, but to her."

Leonie gives a little huff of displeasure.

"I'm not a jealous boyfriend," I say. "It's a matter of safety."

"Fine," she says. "Forward it to me, along with the phone number it came from. I'll see what I can do."

"There's one other thing," I say, remembering something Jaxon mentioned yesterday, which has troubled me ever since. "I want to bring in Olivia's phone at some point, and maybe you can check it for a tracker of some kind."

"That's my favorite kind of job," she says.

I thank Leonie and end the call.

I'll have to explain a phone search to Olivia, but the peace of mind will be worth any of Olivia's misgivings in the end. I don't like the idea of Daniel being able to follow her around, find her so easily. And I suspect some sort of tracker is how he did it.

But wait...maybe the tracker isn't in her phone. Maybe it's in the other item she always has with her.

I go in search of Olivia's handbag. It's in the bedroom, so I upend the contents over the rumpled sheets of Jaxon's bed. A thousand random items tumble out—wallet, phone charger, granola bar, tampons, several tubes of lip gloss, a pack of markers, some condoms. This feels like an invasion of privacy, but I'm not looking at her shit, I'm just trying to find—

There it is. Olivia's phone doesn't have a tracker installed, because the tracker is right here. It's a tiny black device, no larger than one of those circular batteries that belong in smoke detectors. A faint green light blinks on one side.

Fuck. I knew Daniel was an asshole, but this is next-level. We need to get rid of him. And by "get rid of," I mean "put in prison for a long fucking time," but I'd be lying if I said I didn't wish he was dead.

4

Jaxon

My office has been a never-ending parade of applicants that HR sent up to me. These are potential bodyguards who passed the first interview and were rushed up immediately because HR thinks they show promise.

There are many good ones in the mix. There are even a few who are potentially great. Some learned about us from our competitor, because they worked with our team a couple of weeks ago at Olivia's gala. I guess I impressed them, despite that event turning into a shit-show, courtesy of Genevieve.

A woman walks into my office right as my phone buzzes with a text from Ryder. *Call me ASAP. Not emergency, but important.*

I greet the woman, who has medium-brown hair short on one side, buzzed in an undercut on the other.

"Hi, I'm Lin Rosewood," she says. "HR sent me up."

"Jaxon Marsel. Nice to meet you. Give me just a second," I tell her while giving her a brief handshake. "Make yourself comfortable."

I take my phone to the other side of the office to provide a little privacy. Ryder answers immediately. "What's up?" I ask. "Is everything okay?"

"It's fine. But I figured out how Daniel knew where Olivia was—there was a fucking tracker in her purse."

I pinch the bridge of my nose. "Any way to figure out definitively who put it there?"

"Not that I know of. We can ask Leonie to reverse track it, if such a thing is even possible."

"It's worth a shot," I say.

We end the call and I return to my desk. The new applicant is waiting in a chair just in front of it.

"Thanks for waiting, Ms. Rosewood."

"No problem," she says. "Please, call me Lin."

"Lin. You can call me Jaxon."

"Sorry," she says, "but I couldn't help overhearing. Do you need someone tracked?"

"Someone's being tracked, but we wouldn't mind tracking the tracker," I explain. "Why do you ask?"

"Take a look at my resume," she says, gesturing at my computer.

I already have it pulled up, to prepare for her interview. After giving it a quick scan, I look up and meet her green gaze. "You were a private investigator? Shit, before that, you worked on the police force? Detective?"

She nods. "I had to quit to care for a sick parent. The hours were too demanding, the pay not high enough to hire someone else to watch my dad."

We talk some more about Lin's experience, about her

investigative style, and how she sees herself fitting in at Ironwood. She has a few questions about workplace culture, expectations on gathering evidence. She wants to make sure this is a moral company, that there won't be any shady dealings or requests to bend the law. In the end, I'm pleased with her answers and her questions.

"I'd like to hire you," I say. "When can you start?"

"Immediately," she says.

"I have to ask...what was the outcome of you caring for your father? Where is he now?"

She beams. "He fought hard for two years, and he recovered."

"Glad to hear it."

I send Lin down to our investigations department. It's a relatively new department of Ironwood Security. While we need the bodyguards, we could also benefit from more personnel to head some of the bad shit off at the pass, before it reaches us. Someone like Lin, from the looks of her resume, would be a great asset.

Alone in my office, I lean back in my chair. I'm exhausted. Stressed. I miss Olivia with a bone-deep ache. Pulling up my phone, I text her. *Babydoll. What are you up to?*

An incoming video call request comes from Ryder's phone a second later, and I scowl at the screen before answering. But when I click *accept*, it's Olivia's face I see.

"That's a relief," I tell her.

She laughs. "Ryder confiscated my phone. The media won't shut up about the fire at my mom's, and, it's a long story, but some of the stuff they're saying is about me."

I want to knock some sense into the media, but that would be impossible.

"Are you finding other things to do today, then?" I ask.

"Ryder's making me rest." She sticks out her tongue.

"You stick out that tongue, little girl, and I'll come up with some good uses for it."

She leans back on the sofa, her brown locks spreading out behind her on the cushion. "Yeah? I dare you." She sticks out her tongue again.

"What's Ryder doing?" I ask.

"Working."

"At the dining table?" I guess, because that's his favorite spot to set up his laptop.

"Yep."

"Okay, Babydoll. I want you to walk into the dining room."

Looking intrigued and a little uncertain, she does as I tell her. "Okay, I'm here."

"What are you wearing?" I ask.

"Sweatpants and this tank top and sweatshirt." She moves the phone's view so I can get a look at her body, all the way down to her bare toes, covered in a pale pink polish.

"Beautiful," I say. "Lose the sweatshirt and pants. You can give Mr. Ryder his phone back."

She passes the phone to Ryder, who tortures me with a close-up of his nostrils before laughing and swinging the camera back around to point at Olivia. Her gray eyes are dancing with amusement, and she laughs, too.

"Hurry up, Babydoll," I growl.

Her hands tremble slightly as she shucks her clothes until she's wearing only her panties and tank top. I imagine goosebumps cover her skin, but the camera isn't close enough for me to see them.

"Pull out the chair nearest you," I instruct her.

Slowly, she drags it from the table.

"Farther," I say. "Keep going. Good. Now sit in the chair."

If she's wondering why I'm asking this, she doesn't show it. She sits down, her knees pressed together. That won't do.

"Spread your legs for us, gorgeous," I say, getting up from my desk to make sure my office door is locked.

She spreads her legs, and her gray eyes are intent on the camera. Eye contact, just the way she knows I like it.

"Push aside your panties and show me your sweet cunt," I say, my voice low.

With one hand, she pulls her underwear out of the way.

"Fuck," Ryder says. "So fucking hot."

"Hold up your index and middle finger," I say.

Now she looks puzzled, but she complies. "One of those is Mr. Ryder, and the other one is me, Babydoll. Where do you want us?"

She bites her lip. "What do you mean?"

"Where would you take us right now, if you got to pick?"

"In...in my pussy," she says.

"Then put us in there."

With that adorable blush forming over her cheeks, she lowers her fingers to her glistening pussy and slides them inside.

"Does it feel good, baby?" Ryder asks in a rough voice.

"Yes, Sir."

It's fucking torture watching her, not being there. I

wish my cock really was one of those fingers; I can feel pre-come leaking onto my boxers.

"Would you take one of us in your mouth while the other one fucks your pussy?" I ask her.

She nods.

"Good girl," I say. "That would make Daddy so happy, for us both to fuck you again."

Her fingers glisten as she begins to move them in and out of her cunt.

"I bet you taste so good," I say. "Why not let Ryder have a taste?"

She pulls her fingers from her pussy and moves to get up, but Ryder says, "No, little one. Stay right there. I'm coming to you."

He moves right in front of her, then drops to his knees on the floor.

"Hold this for me, princess," he says, handing her the phone.

My view skews momentarily, but then she's pointing the phone at Ryder. He lifts her legs and scoots her ass to the edge of the chair. Then he spreads her folds wide with his fingers and lowers his face, licking along her folds, sucking her clit.

"Oh, fuck," Olivia says, her hips bucking forward.

"Better hold the phone steady," I say. "I called for a show and I want my fucking show."

I can't resist anymore—I hurriedly pull my cock from my pants and stroke and squeeze it. Ryder eats her out like a starving man, groaning as he licks and sucks. He adds fingers. It's killing me to not be there right now, but I plan on doing all of this again with her when I get home.

"Turn the phone around so I can watch your face when you come," I tell her.

The view changes from Ryder eating her pussy and now I'm looking at her gorgeous face.

"Watch me," I instruct her, and she nods. "I'm jacking off right now because I can't fucking stop thinking about you and what it's like to slam my cock inside you. I'm going to come soon, Babydoll. Are you?"

"Yes, Daddy."

"Good. Come for us now."

"Daddy! Mr. Ryder!" she shouts. Her face twists with ecstasy and she shudders with her release, but those beautiful gray eyes never leave mine.

I bring up a hand to catch my own come, because my own relief is right here, my balls tightening, dick harder than should be possible. Come shoots from the tip and I catch it, groaning.

"Fuck, Babydoll," I say. "Thank you, sweetheart. I love you."

"I love you too, Daddy," she whispers, her face slack and sated.

"I've got to go. Have a nice rest."

"Okay. Love you. Bye."

"Rest?" Ryder says, and I catch a glimpse of him shoving his sweats down far enough to free his cock. "If you think you're getting to rest now, little girl, you are sorely mistaken. Bend over this table, now."

I chuckle and end the call, then get myself cleaned up for whatever my work day has to throw at me next. We needed that break, all three of us. I'm only mildly disappointed that I can't be there to continue the scene.

Well, that's what tonight will be for.

Olivia

A few days after the fire, I'm reviewing a list of potential sites for the Youth Arts organization when I spot a listing in the Bellefleur District. *Warehouse, for rent.* It's located in the perfect place—I pull up a map on my laptop to doublecheck. And yep, it's halfway between Wilmington High and Wilmington Middle Schools.

So far, all of the options have been too far from the schools, making them impractical, because kids shouldn't have to be bussed to a program like Youth Arts. It needs to be accessible, not create another hoop for them to jump through.

I re-read the listing. There's no heat in the warehouse, but San Esteban temperatures rarely hit below sixty degrees. The interior is full of machinery, which I can interpret to mean a lot of industrial crap that is out of date and nobody wants. We'll need to get rid of that for safety reasons. The warehouse is a little over three thousand square feet, which is way more than we need, but who knows, we'll have room to grow.

Heart thumping away with hope, I call the contact number for the rental agency.

Ryder

My phone lights up with a text from Olivia. She's in our group chat with Jaxon. *Hey, I found the perfect place!*

Jaxon responds before I can finish my congratulatory text. *Well done! Where is it?*

She responds, *It's on Caro, close to both schools!!!*

Congratulations, I write. *But isn't that in the Bellefleur District?*

Kind of the point, she writes back. *That's where both Wilmington schools are.*

I frown at my phone. Bellefleur is decidedly sketchy. Jaxon and I have focused a lot of our charitable efforts on the area, but it's still rife with crime. And Olivia wants to station herself there, of all places?

Another text flashes on my screen, from Jaxon. The message is just between us, so Olivia won't see it. *I don't like this.*

Yeah, neither do I, I write back.

I'm going to check it out now, Olivia writes next, in our group chat.

Wait for one of us to come with you, I say.

Already on my way. I have Terrence and Roman.

Dammit. Even when she has bodyguards, I don't feel great about this.

Jaxon's form darkens my doorway and he says, "I'm concerned."

I text Olivia. *Can we talk about this before you go?*

Sorry. Already on my way.

I'm not asking you not to go. I just want to talk first.

She doesn't respond.

Jaxon's eyes darken as he glowers at his phone. "The fuck?" he mutters.

A message from him pops up in the group text. *We need to talk, Olivia.*

No response.

"I'm texting Roman," I say. *Checking in. Everything okay?*

Roman's response is immediate. *All is well.* It's followed with his personal security code, a string of numbers to reassure us that it's actually him responding.

So now Olivia is ignoring us.

I meet Jaxon's gaze. "I think we have a disobedient brat on our hands."

He nods. "Let's meet her at home, shall we?"

My hand is itching to give her our special kind of discipline. A spanking to turn her ass red and show her who's boss, and a good fucking to remind her that we want her. Followed by cuddling and making up so that she knows we love her.

5

Olivia

The warehouse is perfect. The woman from the rental agency allows me as much time as I want to poke around both inside and outside the building.

The outside is covered in graffiti, which we'll need to paint over. Maybe, eventually, we'll have enough young artists here that we can plan out and create a mural to discourage future graffiti. Trash litters the sidewalk outside, and an ugly chain-link fence separates the building and its dirt parking lot from Caro Boulevard and its noisy traffic. A couple of tarps are suspended from the other side of the fence, making a flimsy shelter for unhoused people along the sidewalk.

Inside the warehouse, there are two large restrooms with multiple stalls, as well as a break room with a stove and a spot for a refrigerator. While the focus will be art, I want to make sure these kids are fed, too.

Three thousand square feet is a lot of space, and I'm looking over it all, imagining drafting tables, pottery wheels, easels, and more. I can imagine circles of chairs where a volunteer shares their expertise on something like photography, color, composition, or even something like art history, to give students a foundation in the classics. Maybe the students could riff off of old themes or take a composition and make it new, applicable to their modern world.

Chills erupt over my skin at the presence of all of this potential.

The woman from the rental agency sneaks a glance at her watch, and I realize I've spent almost an hour here.

"I should let you get going," I say, walking to the door. Roman and Terrence have been shadowing me, their eyes watchful for danger this entire time. But there's been no danger, because I can feel it deep in my soul—this is the right spot for the Youth Arts program. "I'd love to see a rental application with an explanation of all terms and any zoning issues I should be aware of."

"I'll email it to you as soon as I get back to the office," she says, beaming.

I'm practically bouncing up and down in excitement as Terrence, Roman, and I make our way back to the car. This place is going to be perfect.

Jaxon and Ryder aren't going to think so. As soon as Ryder asked about the Bellefleur District, I could practically feel waves of his disapproval coming through my phone. But this is my project, not theirs. If I wanted to help already-privileged rich kids, then I'd find somewhere in a "respectable" neighborhood.

Well, they might disapprove, but ultimately, the decision is mine.

I can't even bring myself to look at my phone once I'm safely tucked in the backseat of the car, though. I don't want their paranoia to diminish my good feelings about this. I wish I could share the news with them, though—share the perfection of the warehouse and its location, amenities, size, everything.

I also can't handle going through the next years knowing they hate my decision. Maybe if I soften it for them somehow...I could make them a meal while I share everything. A man's heart is through his stomach. Isn't that how the saying goes? There's still two to three hours before they get back to the penthouse after work. Thank goodness they've stopped taking turns to babysit me. I loved the attention, but I was also starting to feel a little *too* protected.

"Hey, can we stop at a grocery store?" I ask Terrence, who's driving.

"Sure thing, Ms. Santiago."

"Olivia," I say.

"No, Olivia's not my name. You can call me Terrence," he says, smirking.

Roman laughs, and I do, too.

I can't remember ever getting a bodyguard to call me *Olivia*, and now it's a long-running joke between us all.

I gather the necessary food for a steak stir-fry that I've just looked up on my phone. I'm not a great cook. Not even a good one. But it's the thought that counts, right? And this recipe looks easy enough for me to manage. The guys will be so impressed, they'll overlook what they no doubt will believe to be my questionable judgment in a site for the Youth Arts program.

I'm left to carry the grocery bags because Terrence and Roman are supposed to keep their arms free in case of danger. They walk with me to the elevator and climb in with me, and we ride up to the penthouse, where the doors slide open.

I'm expecting an empty apartment so I can get to work figuring out this whole cooking thing, but instead, Jaxon is standing right in front of the elevator doors.

I step forward, gulping, and the doors whoosh shut behind me, taking Terrence and Roman back to the parking garage.

"You ignored our texts and calls, Babydoll," Jaxon says, his brown eyes dark with anger.

Ryder approaches from the living room to standing next to Jaxon, his arms folded across his chest.

Oh, shit.

Ryder

Olivia's eyes go wide with surprise. "Oh," she says, a strain in her voice. "You're home already."

"Yep," I say.

"I was…I was going to make dinner. I wanted to surprise you two." She holds up two canvas totes, full of food.

"You can cook?" Jaxon asks.

She blushes. "Not really. I mean, not well. But I wanted to do something nice."

"To butter us up?" I ask. "Because you knew we'd be angry with you?"

A soft intake of breath. Yeah, she knows we caught her. I'm half-angry, half-aroused, because I know in a few minutes, my palm will be warming her ass.

"Well, I didn't *know* you'd be angry," she hedges.

"You might have, if you bothered looking at your texts," Jaxon says, "but I'm guessing you haven't done that."

She presses her lips together, shakes her head. "No. I didn't want you to tell me not to go. You should see the warehouse, you guys—it's absolutely perfect..." She trails off at the stern expression on Jaxon's face.

"The perfection of the warehouse isn't what's under question here," I say.

"Of course not." She frowns. "What's under question is the safety of it, or whatever."

"Or *whatever*?" Jaxon says, his eyebrows shooting up on his forehead.

"And no, that's not what's under question," I say. "What we have a problem with is you ignoring us when all we wanted to do was discuss things."

"You wanted me to stay out of Bellefleur," she whispers.

"No. We wanted to talk," Jaxon says.

I move toward her and cup her chin in my hand before pressing a kiss to her soft lips. I reach down and take the grocery bags from her hands and carry them to the kitchen. "Get naked, Babydoll," I say over my shoulder. "Jax and I have plans for you."

"I should put those things away," she says. "Some

should be frozen or refrigerated if we're not going to use them right now."

"I'll take care of it," I say.

"Naked, Olivia," Jaxon says. "Now."

The sounds of her clothing shifting around reach my ears and I grin to myself. I'm still pissed, but our little girl's going to see the error of her ways. I quickly put away any perishable items and leave the rest on the counter for later. When I return to the living room, Olivia is completely naked, her clothes in a heap on the floor.

"Crawl to the bedroom," Jax tells her.

She gives him a sullen look. "I don't see that what I did deserves this kind of treatment."

"Really?" he says. "Ignoring your daddies when we asked for a simple conversation about your safety? You don't see a problem with that? Ryder, man, I don't know if a simple spanking is going to cut it with this bratty little girl."

She drops to her hands and knees and begins to crawl to the bedroom. Jaxon falls into step, moving slowly next to her, then he reaches down and grabs a bunch of her hair in his hand, wrapping it around his fist so it works as a leash. It's long enough he can do it without hurting her.

"What are you—Jaxon, this is embarrassing," she says.

"Good."

Her sumptuous ass is a temptation as she makes her way to the bedroom. I want to stop her and mount her just like this, shove my cock into her pussy—which is already glistening with arousal. She might be embarrassed or feel slightly demeaned by having to crawl, but she gets off on it.

Just like we do.

"Stand up and brace your arms on the foot of the bed," Jaxon tells her, letting go of her hair.

She does as he asks. Her breasts hang down, swaying slightly as she moves. Her nipples are hard little points and I yearn to take one in my mouth.

"You're going to take your spankings, and then we're going to talk," Jaxon says.

"Not fuck?" Olivia asks.

"Not yet," Jaxon says.

"Maybe not at all, if you don't obey us," I say.

She sniffs. "I'm obeying."

Jaxon and I share a look. She's obeying, but she's not submitting.

The scene isn't right.

"Forget it," I say, taking a step back.

"What?" Olivia asks, turning to look at me over her shoulder.

"I'm not doing this," I say. "It's not going to work."

"Yeah, same," Jaxon says.

Olivia frowns, her brows coming together in confusion. "What are you going to do?"

"Whatever the fuck we feel like, I guess," I say.

Her frown grows more pronounced. "And what am I going to do?"

"Same thing," Jax says. "Whatever the fuck you feel like."

"Shouldn't we talk?" Olivia asks. "About, you know, this afternoon?"

"Do you even want to?" I ask.

She doesn't budge from her place over the bed, even though her legs are shaking slightly. "I don't want to, but don't you think we should? I know you're upset, and. Crap. I get it, okay?"

"What do you get?" I ask.

Her beautiful gray eyes fill with tears, but she blinks them back. "If all you wanted to do was talk to me about safety, the least I could've done was allow it. But I thought you'd forbid me from going to Bellefleur, and the place really is perfect, and I didn't want you to tell me I couldn't do it."

"Olivia, sweetheart, when have we ever forbidden you from anything?" Jaxon steps forward and puts his hand on her lower back, soothing her as he speaks.

Taking a deep, shuddering breath, she says, "I'm sorry, Daddy. I'm sorry, Sir."

Immediately I move to her other side and start to pull her up.

"No," she says, "I think you should punish me. I was terrible to you both."

My hands still on her shoulders. "You're saying you *want* a spanking?"

She nods.

Well, this is good news to me, because I want to give her a spanking. Sitting down on the edge of the bed, I say, "Come over here, baby girl, and lie across my lap."

While she moves into position, I look up at Jaxon. His eyes are dark, his arms folded across his chest.

"Olivia," he says, "do you understand why you're being punished right now?"

"Yes." She nods, her soft form shaking slightly over my legs.

"Do you trust us?" he asks.

She takes a deep, shuddering breath. "Yes."

"Do you trust that we want you always?"

Silence.

"Olivia?" I ask.

"I'm trying," she whispers.

I look over at Jaxon and shrug. She's trying. His expression is closed off, but I can sense his disappointment, because I feel it, too. When we met Olivia, she had just ended things with Daniel. He'd truly fucked with her head.

"Trying is good," Jaxon says. "In the meantime, you will accept our punishments when you've been naughty."

"Yes, Daddy." Her voice is quiet.

I don't give her any warning—I bring my hand down in a sharp smack on her ass.

"Ouch," Olivia says on an exhale, but there's no real pain there. Not yet.

Jaxon leans against the wall, eyes glittering.

I bring my hand down again, feel the sting in my palm. Olivia kicks up one of her legs, her ass and thighs jiggling deliciously as she tries to get out of my grasp.

"Are you trying to escape, little girl?" I ask her.

"No, Sir," she says, stilling her movements.

Sir again. I'm getting pretty fucking tired of *Sir* and *Mr. Ryder*.

I spank her again and again, until her cheeks are bright red with heat. I massage them while she hisses at the pain, before moving a single finger down to her pussy. She's soaking wet. Grinning at Jax, I pull my finger away and show him just how much that spanking got her going.

"Submission is so much better than begrudging acceptance, isn't it, princess?" I ask, putting my finger back against her folds and spreading her slickness around.

Olivia moans. "Yes, Sir."

"And we'll talk about the warehouse in Bellefleur later," I continue, "and how you can trust us to listen when you have an opinion on anything. But right now I want to eat this pussy, so lie down on the bed for me."

"On my back?" she asks, her hands going to cover her butt.

Jaxon chuckles. "Yes, on your back. I'm going to fuck your naughty mouth while he eats you, sweetheart. Let your head hang over the edge, here."

"Ow, ow, ow," she says as she gets into position. Her ass must be burning from the good spanking I gave her.

"Wide open, princess. Show me everything," I say, pushing her knees apart.

She doesn't trust us to talk things through? Right here, right now, we'll remind her that she can trust us with her body. If that's what it takes to show her how things work for us, then that's what we'll do.

6

Olivia

Ryder presses his mouth against my pussy and I nearly fly off of the bed. Warm heat and gentle suction, and his hands press my thighs apart, holding me in place so I can't wiggle around and try to direct things. No, he's in control, and he's the boss.

He's not the only boss, though—Jaxon has pulled his cock from his pants. I'm looking at it upside down, my head draped over the bed's edge. From any angle, Jaxon's cock is magnificent, jutting proudly from dark, curly hair. I know what kind of pleasure it can give me, and I know what kind of domination and punishment it can dole out.

Right now, he angles it toward my lips and runs the head over them. I open my mouth and lick the tip. Jaxon groans.

"Open wide, Babydoll," he says.

My brain doesn't know what to focus on—the wet sucking of Ryder's lips and tongue against my clit and pussy, or the confident way Jaxon strokes his cock into my mouth. He goes in so far, I worry about my gag reflex, but then he's pulling back out, allowing me to breathe.

"You okay, baby?" he asks.

I make an affirmative sound, unable to speak, and he begins to rhythmically stroke in and out of my mouth. I cup my tongue around his shaft, swirling it as much as I can despite not having a lot of room to work. I'm getting into it, focusing more on Jaxon and loving the way he swears a stream of brutal, filthy words. He brings his hands down to play with my breasts.

And then Ryder pushes two fingers into my pussy. He crooks them toward the front, hitting my g-spot. The orgasm hits fast and hard, and I cry out around Jaxon's cock.

Ryder licks me through it, slowing the stroke of his fingers. Jaxon lightly pinches both of my nipples at the same time, reminding me to keep focusing on him. I'm vaguely aware of Ryder moving away from my legs, but he's back a moment later. I can't see what he's doing; I can only feel the heat of him between my thighs.

"Hold her ankles for me," he says to Jaxon, and they lift my legs.

Ryder moves his cock between my pussy folds, then takes it away. I make a noise of disappointment. Jaxon smooths a hand over my ankle. "Don't worry, he's coming back to you, little one."

Something warm and wet touches my ass, sliding between my spread cheeks. That was not where I expected Ryder to go. I'm tempted to tap Jaxon's leg to tell him I need a time out so I can ask what Ryder thinks he's doing...but I trust these guys to know.

I trust them.

I should've trusted them when it came to talking about the warehouse in Bellefleur, I realize.

Crap. That's what they were talking about. I was an idiot.

There's no way to apologize now, not with my mouth crammed full and Jaxon's scent and taste filling my senses.

The head of Ryder's cock stops at my back entrance. He exerts a tiny bit of pressure.

"Relax, princess. I'll make it good for both of us," he says in a strangled voice.

I breathe out and relax my muscles. Jaxon's hands are firm on my ankles, holding up my legs. He brings them lower, so my knees are close to my shoulders. Holy hell, I had no idea my body could fold up like this.

And then Ryder presses inside.

I moan loudly at the feeling of fullness, the forbidden intrusion, the way my body stretches to accommodate his girth.

"You're being so good for us, princess," he croons, spreading my ass cheeks with his hands and making them sting from my earlier spanking.

The pain mixes with the pressure of his advancing cock, and my blood turns hotter in my veins. A powerful orgasm is shimmering on the horizon and all I have to do is wait and my men will give it to me.

I lose all sense of time and give in to the men. My body is theirs. My heart is theirs. Ryder's voice is a deep rasp as he praises me while keeping a hard rhythm of thrusting. Jaxon lets go of one of my legs so he can touch my cheek and he, too, tells me what a beautiful, good girl

I am. Their words are as good as their rough-yet-gentle touches.

Reaching around my legs, Ryder grips one of my breasts and begins to ruthlessly tweak the nipple, pinching, flicking, pulling, twisting it. My moans increase in volume—I couldn't hold them back if I wanted to—and Jaxon's thrusts become harsh, frenetic.

"Touch your clit, Babydoll," Jaxon says. "Come for your daddies. Come for us now."

A quick rub against my clit, and I come apart, my need and ecstasy exploding throughout my body, all heat, all joy. Jaxon empties down my throat and I drink him down. Ryder roars as he comes, slamming his cock into me so I feel his thighs against my ass.

Jaxon pulls out of my mouth and cradles the back of my head, and Ryder pulls out and helps lower my legs to the bed.

"Shower time, little one," Ryder says.

"Only if you're coming with me," I say. The shower is big enough for all three of us, and I let them wash me, their movements full of care.

Once we're out of the shower, Jaxon wraps me in a robe and Ryder grabs the leave-in conditioner and a comb.

"Now we talk," Ryder says.

My shoulders fall. It's shitty to have to admit I'm wrong. But I need to do it.

∾

Jaxon

I can tell the last thing Olivia wants to do is talk to us about this, but it's important. We're doing something wrong if we haven't earned her trust, and I need to figure out what it is.

The three of us make our way to the kitchen. "I'll cook while Ryder combs your hair," I say.

Ryder laughs. "Um, no. I'm not letting you cook—you're the worst."

"Fine." I hold up my hands, because he has a point.

Olivia's eyes dance briefly with merriment before she grows more subdued again. "I was going to cook for you both."

"Another time." Ryder wraps an arm around her shoulders, squeezes her tight, and presses a smacking kiss on her cheek.

I take the comb and conditioner from him, settle Olivia onto one of the stools against the kitchen island, and begin combing the tangles from her hair.

"Oh, that feels amazing," Olivia moans, tilting her head back slightly. "This is the best."

"The best, huh?" I ask, cupping her cheek as I'd done while I was fucking her mouth.

She gives me a flirtatious wink. "Maybe not the *best* best."

Ryder gathers ingredients and starts cooking, but his back is never turned to us for long. "So, Babydoll. You thought we'd forbid you from going to the Bellefleur district."

Her shoulders rise as she takes a deep breath. "I was stupid, and I'm sorry."

"Not stupid," I say, easing the comb through a tricky tangle of hair. "I need you to know that just because you're our babydoll, doesn't mean you don't get a voice. You're still an adult woman, and we all recognize that, you know?"

"I know," she says quietly. "I just didn't want you to be mad at me, or disappointed in my choice."

"We just wanted to talk," I say.

"And speaking of that," Ryder says, "there's something I've been holding back."

She turns her head sharply to look at him. "What?"

"It's a couple of things. One, Daniel sent a message to your phone while I was monitoring your texts."

Olivia cocks her head at him. She's not angry, and I love that about her, because she could so easily fly off the handle and be pissed. But instead, she's waiting for the full explanation. "What did he say? In the text?"

"He warned you to be careful." Ryder scowls. "And he sent a video of him destroying your sculptures."

Her sharp intake of breath is the only reaction from her. I want to hold her, but I don't want to distract her from the conversation. "You were watching my phone a few days ago," she says finally. "Why are you just telling me about this now?"

"It was that same day as all the news segments and articles suggesting you were behind the fire," I say, touching her arm.

"I really don't like that you kept it from me," she says. "I understand why, but...I hate being left out. If you want me to act like an adult and communicate, well, that goes both ways."

She makes a great point.

"We just want to protect you," I say. "But you're also right, that we need to talk more."

"Yes, apparently we do." She rolls her head around, as if trying to relieve tension. "Ryder, you said there were a couple of things?"

"Right." He does something with the food on the stove, then turns around to face us again. "The second thing is I found a tracker in your purse."

"You were rifling through my purse?" Her voice rises at the end.

Ryder holds out his hands. "Not really. I mean, I did, but not to snoop. But I was wondering how Daniel could've found you at your mom's house. I wasn't sure how to tell you either of these things, but I think you should know. We probably seem overprotective, but shit like that is partly the reason for it."

Nodding, she says, "I get it. I don't love it, but I get it. I can't believe...no, of course I can believe he would do something like that. A tracker. It's so...I mean, I can't be *that* important to him."

"You definitely can," I say. "He's sick, sweetheart. To him, I suspect his behavior seems normal."

"I had Leonie try to reverse-track it," Ryder says. "The results were confusing."

"Confusing how?" I ask, because this is news to me—I didn't realize Leonie had finished her work on the tracker.

"The signal was pinging from somewhere fairly far north of here, in Kinasey County."

"Kinasey County?" Olivia says. "That's weird. It sounds familiar for some reason."

"Anything to do with Daniel?" Ryder asks.

"No, I don't think so."

Ryder shrugs. "Well, as far as we know, Daniel's family doesn't have any properties up that way, and we've been assuming he would hide out somewhere familiar." Turning around to mess with things on the stove again, Ryder says, "Anyway, we're still trying to put things together, and when we have more info, we'll share it, okay?"

"Okay." Olivia shakes her body, as if trying to clear Daniel and the tracker from her mind. "As far as that warehouse, you're not angry?"

"No, we're not angry," I say. "You know, Babydoll, you don't have to fear conflict with us."

I want to growl the words and look into her eyes, but I can guess that would come off as too aggressive right now. So instead, I calmly drag the comb through her wet hair, watching the water spots it leaves on her robe.

"I know that, it's just hard to put it into practice," she says.

Ryder adds greens to the stir-fry he's making, then he turns around and faces us, spatula in hand. "Is there anything Jax and I can do to make it easier on you to believe and act on?"

"I don't know." She shrugs. "I don't think so. I guess I just need time."

"I guess now's as good of a time as any to say I really don't care how long you keep that studio apartment," I tell her, squeezing her shoulder and trying to ease some of the tension she's holding there. "Whenever you're ready. Just please be honest with us. We have to communicate."

"Okay," she says, turning to give me a tentative smile.

I kiss her mouth once, twice, then again, and I lean back until she smiles once more—this time fully.

Jaxon

After dinner, Ryder and I climb into bed with Olivia and wait until she's fast asleep. Then Ryder catches my eye. "Drink?"

I don't want to leave Olivia for even a moment, but I need to talk out some of the bad shit in my head, so I shrug. "Sure."

"Meet you in the living room," he says, and takes off.

I throw on a pair of pajama pants, and find Ryder in the living room. He's thrown on a pair of sweatpants and grabbed a bottle of whiskey and two glasses. After pouring, he hands me a glass and takes the other, and we sit on different sofas.

"Something's on your mind," he says.

I nod and take a sip. The sensation of the alcohol going down my throat reminds me to relax my muscles, and I sigh. "Yeah. It's getting to me that she's having a hard time believing in us."

"You need to get over that," he says.

"Why? Why do I need to get over it?"

"We've talked about this." He takes a sip of his whiskey and sighs. "She's on a different...wavelength? Timetable? I don't know. She's in a different place, coming from a different place."

A flash of anger comes over me at the thought of what her asshole ex put her through. Domestic violence is no joke. Pissed at him, and wanting to help Olivia, and wanting our relationship to be where I'm at with it, for all of us, I say, "What does she need, a marriage proposal? Because I'll fucking do it, man."

The words hang between us, caught in the static tension of the moment.

"You're ready for that, huh?" he asks. "Even after what Gen—"

"I don't even want to hear her name anymore. Yes. Olivia is an entirely different person."

"Fuck, I know that," he says, scowling. "I'm just surprised, is all."

I sigh and rub my face. The sweet taste of Olivia's kiss goodnight is still on my lips, more potent than whiskey. "Are you not there yet?"

He laughs. "I've been there. As soon as I got over my hang-ups about betraying you, I was all in. Do you think she would have us? Will she even believe we want her forever?"

"I don't know. I haven't thought it through. But I know what I want, and it's good to know you're on the same page."

"Yeah." He nods in a resolute sort of way. "We have her for now. Now we need to get her to agree to forever."

Olivia

A few days pass. The days are getting shorter, and although San Esteban never gets cold, I can feel a differ-ence in the air. I put up a job posting, seeking part-time and full-time employees for the organization. We have more than enough to pay people, and while it would be great to run it on volunteers, I want to get a core staff assembled to run it.

And the best news is that Jaxon and Ryder approve of the location. They don't love the district, but I have two bodyguards and they judge it safe enough, as long as I don't go alone.

Caro Boulevard stretches through the Bellefleur district and into Dorado Heights, where Jaxon's penthouse is located. I'm coming from the warehouse, where I've just picked up the keys and security info from the rental agent. My heart thumps happily in my chest, because this is fucking happening.

Squid's at the wheel and Cora's riding shotgun. The rundown buildings of Bellefleur are in our wake, and upscale boutiques and grocery stores now fill the blocks ahead. I spot a shop sign. *Morgan's Jewelry – Custom and Unique Pieces*. Beneath the sign is smaller print which reads *Engraving and Personalization Available*.

Fingering the necklace Jaxon gave me, I say, "Can we stop for a minute, please?"

"Sure thing, Ms. Santiago," Squid says.

"Olivia," I mutter under my breath, but I know it's useless at this point.

Squid quickly finds us a parking spot at the curb. I envy his parallel parking skills.

In fact, I envy him his driving skills. If I don't get behind the wheel again one of these days, I'm going to completely forget how to drive.

I go into the shop, and Squid and Cora follow close behind.

A woman with an explosion of curly brown hair sits at the counter, examining a ring through a magnifying glass. She looks up as I approach. "Hello, can I help you?"

Running the charm back and forth on my necklace chain, I say, "Hi. I was wondering about getting something engraved."

"Sure thing," she says with a smile. "Depending on the simplicity of the design, I might be able to do it while you wait."

7

Olivia

My auburn wig is in place and my make-up is heavy. I'm going to go insane if I have to spend another day working inside the penthouse. I love the place, truly, but I am craving something full of carbs and the kind of sugary coffee that'll feel like it's immediately rotting my teeth.

Although the media interest in the fire at my mom's has died down, journalists are still whispering about what my role was in the event. I set my phone to only ring when people in my contacts list call me, so at least I'm not having to deal with interruptions.

I just need out of the house.

Cora and Hunter are my guards today. Both of them are fairly reserved, so our drive to my favorite café is quiet. Which means when my phone blares with my mom's ringtone, "Barracuda," programmed in there by

Samantha, I jump at the sudden loudness and rush to answer.

"Hey," I say.

"Darling," she says.

Oh, shit. She never leads with *darling* unless she wants something.

"What's up?" I ask. "Have you found a contractor for the guest house?"

"Yes, of course," she says briskly. "It'll be good as new in no time."

"That's great."

An awkward pause stretches between us, and I count the number of dogs we pass as Cora drives us down the block. San Esteban's dog owners are out in force today, probably because it's so beautiful outside.

"Listen," Mom says, "I know that we haven't really talked since the fire. I haven't called as often as I should."

To be fair, I haven't made myself available, either. I'm afraid she's going to bring up my relationship with Jaxon and Ryder, and I don't want to have that conversation, while at the same time knowing it would be better to just get it out of the way.

"I hate that the media was saying those things about you," she continues. "And I got to thinking, it might be really good for your image—and mine—if you were to come to an event on Sunday afternoon."

I feel a bubbling of anger in my heart. This isn't about my image at all—it's about her. It always is, always has been. "An event?"

"A town hall sort of meeting, up north. Some of my constituents up there are upset about the black-eared fox protections I'm trying to implement."

If I never hear about the black-eared fox again, it will be too soon. "I'm busy," I say. "Sorry, I can't make it."

She takes a breath, probably to argue, but I speak first. "I know it's important to your optics, but I have a life outside of your politics, Mom."

"I know," she says with a little sigh. "It's terrible, but sometimes I miss when I could just put you into a pretty dress and you'd smile at everyone. The media loved your pretty—"

"Gray eyes, yeah, I know," I say. I've heard this a thousand times. "They certainly don't like my pretty gray eyes now. Last I heard, someone from KSC News said my gray eyes look vacant and crazy."

"Yes, well, nobody listens to KSC News."

Some people must, or it wouldn't be on the air. But I don't say that. Cora's parking close to my café, and I have work to do, my own life to live.

"I gotta go, Mom."

"All right. Call me soon to set up brunch. We still need to have that talk."

"Okay. Talk to you soon." I can't get off the phone fast enough.

"I love you, Olivia." Her voice sounds strained.

"Love you, too."

I hang up and stare at my phone screen until it goes black. I wonder why she sounded so weird. Trouble with work? I almost feel bad for telling her I couldn't go to her town hall or whatever it was. But look at me—I'm already wearing a wig and heavy make-up in the hopes that the media won't recognize me at a café in downtown San Esteban. Why would I voluntarily place myself in the media's sights?

Cora and Hunter give the coffee shop a sweep, their professional gazes assessing and careful. They're treating downtown like a war zone full of hostile soldiers, but after what happened at my mom's house, who can blame them?

But the coffee shop is nothing like a war zone. The place is a little more than half-full, with the tables taken up by people chatting or zoning out to work on their laptops and phones. Faint music plays in the background, something in a language I don't know, with a jazzy old feel to it. The paintings on the walls are all colorful abstracts. Most of them aren't to my taste, but I do love the bright colors.

Once I have a chocolate croissant and a sugary caffeinated drink (complete with whipped cream and sprinkles, because of course), I park myself at a table and pull my tablet from my handbag.

4Hire is the app I'm using to screen applicants. Jaxon recommended it, saying if Youth Arts didn't have the budget for me to pay the fees, he'd cover them himself. I tap on the little icon and a notification in the corner alerts me to the fact that I have six applicants. Not bad, I think, grinning to myself and taking a sip of my drink.

The noise of the café fades into the background while I begin looking over applications. The first one, I can rule out immediately. The applicant left half of the questions blank.

I stretch out, nudging the chair across from me back a little bit so I can put my feet up in the seat.

Halfway through reading the second application, which is showing some real promise, a guy walks past my table. The toe of his shoe hooks on the ornate, wrought-iron foot of the chair opposite me, where my feet are resting, and he stumbles. Hot coffee spills down the front of his shirt and he groans.

I jump up, napkins already in hand. "Here, take these."

He gives me a sheepish smile. "Thanks. I can't believe I did that. My boss is already looking for an excuse to fire me, and now I'm going to be late."

"Go get cleaned up," I tell him. "I'll put in another order for you."

"Really?"

"Yeah. What's the drink?"

"A large decaf soy latte. Thanks." He reaches for his wallet, but I wave him off.

"I got it," I say. "Least I can do, for pushing my chair out like a menace."

He chuckles and wanders toward the restrooms. Cora and Hunter, who've been sitting at the table next to mine, give the guy a good stare.

"Oh, he's fine," I tell them. "Watch my stuff?"

Hunter grumbles about being less concerned about my stuff than he is about weirdos attacking my person, but Cora nods and gestures with her chin that Hunter can follow me to the counter.

I put in the guy's order and pay for it, feeling bad for pushing out that chair. Poor guy. I hope his boss doesn't get mad at him.

"Actually," I tell the barista, "can I get one of those chocolate chip cookies, too?"

By the time she's done ringing me up, the guy has emerged from the restroom, his dark gray shirt completely soaked on the front, but at least not stained that I can tell.

"I'm so sorry," I say again.

He grins and shakes his head. He has a goatee, and an eyebrow ring which catches the light while he shakes his head. "It's all right. No harm done."

"Yet," I say. "I hope you don't get in trouble. Here's an apology cookie, to go with the coffee. You can eat it yourself, or give it to your boss."

"Thanks. Maybe I'll eat it. I need to hang out for a few minutes and let my shirt dry out."

I feel bad all over again. The tables are fairly full. "You can sit with me," I offer.

Hunter gives me a dirty look—he obviously doesn't trust this stranger. I don't have to trust him to let him sit down in a public place, so I just shrug and point the guy to the chair that tripped him.

"Thanks," he says, settling in. "I won't disturb you for long, promise. I can see you're working."

"Yeah, I'm—" I pause. I can't trust him or give him any real information on myself. Hunter's still glaring daggers at the guy and even Cora's giving him the side-eye. For all I know, this man could be a journalist. "I'm a little busy," I hedge.

"How busy?" He gives me a flirtatious smile. Wow, that came on fast. "Too busy to let me take you out to dinner sometime?"

"Um...yeah," I say. "I have a boyfriend." Two, actually, but he doesn't need to know that.

"Lucky man," the guy says, pulling his shirt from his chest in an attempt to air it out.

"Thanks," I say awkwardly, not knowing what else to say.

After a minute that feels like an hour, he stands up. "I should get going."

I gasp when he reaches for me and lean back in my chair.

Cora stands up quickly, ready to come to my defense. The guy holds up his hands in a *no harm* gesture. "I was just going to shake your hand."

I give a nervous laugh. "I'm a little skittish."

His gaze flicks from me to the bodyguards, then back again. "Sorry, you must be pretty important. I didn't mean to alarm anyone."

"Thanks." I give him a tight smile.

"I'll be going," he says. "Thanks for replacing my coffee, and for the cookie."

"No problem," I say. "Good luck with work."

He lifts the coffee cup in a wordless salute, and then he's out of the shop. It takes a few minutes for my heart-beat to return to normal. Hot tears fill my eyes, but I blink them away. I just wanted to pretend to be normal again for a little while. But what I used to consider a throw-away, mundane interaction in a café has transformed into an Event with a capital E, full of danger.

"Ms. Santiago, are you all right?" Cora asks.

I take a deep breath. "Yep, I'm fine. I think I'm ready to go back to the penthouse, though."

So much for my big adventure out in the world, reclaiming my safety and security.

⁓

Ryder

When I get into the penthouse that evening, Olivia is sitting on the sofa facing the elevator, scowling at her e-reader.

"Hey, baby girl," I say, dropping my wallet, keys, and phone on the side table next to the elevator door. "How was your day?"

"It was fine," she says, turning that scowl on me briefly before going back to whatever she's reading.

Weird. She usually jumps up for a hug.

"Is something wrong?" I ask.

"No, why does something have to be wrong?" Her voice is full of attitude.

Bad mood. I wonder what put her there, and whether I can get her out of it. "Don't use that tone of voice with me, princess."

She curls her lip in annoyance, and now *I* am getting annoyed. I'd love to force her to get into the mood for some fun, so she could relax and be happy. But there's only so much dominance can accomplish. If she's just not into it, she's just not into it. I know how to read a room.

But I also know Olivia, and I know what she likes.

So I go to my room and change out of my slacks and work shirt, and put on a pair of faded gray sweatpants. I leave my chest bare and pad back out to the living room, carrying a book.

She does a double-take when I sit down on the other couch, and her eyes get wider with interest at the sight of me dressed like this. I don't know why, but these pants seem to do something for her.

"Why are you way over on the other sofa?" she asks.

"Giving you space," I say, opening my book and pretending to read.

"Good," she huffs.

I manage to keep a straight face, but it's hard when I want to grin, because she keeps shooting looks over at me while she pretends to read. After a few minutes, she gives a big sigh and tosses her e-reader down in disgust even while she peeks over at me from beneath her eyelashes.

Now, I know it's okay to play.

"Pick up your e-reader, Babydoll," I say.

"I don't think I will," she says, standing and stretching.

My dick starts to get hard and I drawl, "If you can't obey, I'll make you obey."

"Psh. I'd like to see you try."

I toss my own book aside and I'm in front of her in half a second, holding her back to my front. I press my cock against the swell of her ass, seeking the perfect relief I can only find in the heat of her body. "You're on thin ice, little girl."

"I don't know," she gasps. "It feels rather...*thick*...to me." She arches her back, pressing her ass harder against my cock.

Fuck. This isn't going to be slow or controlled. I can't control myself, not right now. She's brought out the sadistic disciplinarian within me and I need to fucking dominate her in the sort of way that will get us both off as fast as possible.

"Go over to the windows," I say.

She shakes her head.

"Move your ass, Babydoll. Now."

She moves it by rubbing it against my cock.

"You know very well that's not what I meant," I say, wrapping her ponytail around my hand. Keeping my fist close to her head, so I don't pull her hair too hard, I push her down until she has to bend over, then I start leading her toward the windows.

"Mr. Ryder," she gasps, "it's scary when I think anyone could be watching."

"But you like it, you dirty little thing," I say.

She doesn't have a comeback. I wait a moment longer, waiting for a safe word, which she also doesn't give me. Then I walk her the rest of the way to the window. I yank off her shirt, none too gently, then shove down her pants and underwear. She moves to kick them away, but I say, "No, leave them right there. This is going to be so tight, you'll feel me tomorrow."

Her lacy bra is still on, and I consider leaving it that way, but I like the idea of her nipples pressed against the glass too much, so I undo the snaps and let the bra fall.

"Hands on the glass, princess," I say, and when she doesn't move, I give her ass a swat. "You are just begging for punishment, aren't you?"

"So what if I am?" she asks in a bratty voice.

I pull my hand back and spank her again, loving the way her ass jiggles slightly with the hit, and the way she gasps at the sting. A second later, my handprint starts to form on her skin.

Slowly, she puts her hands on the window.

"There we go," I say, smoothing my hand over the marks on her ass cheeks. "Are you ready to be a good girl?"

"No," she says.

I give her another swat, and she gasps, pushing up onto her tiptoes.

"I'll keep spanking you, then, until you're ready," I murmur, biting gently down on the shell of her ear.

"Fuck you," she says.

"Oh, you will, Babydoll. You will."

I spank her several more times, until her ass is truly red and she's gasping and moaning, moving her thighs back and forth in a futile attempt to get some friction on her pussy.

"Are you ready to be a good girl for me?" I grab her ponytail again and use it to turn her head so she's facing me.

Her pupils are blown out like she's high, her lips parted. She licks her lower lip and tries to angle her head for a kiss. She looks blissed out.

"There's my sweet girl," I say, giving her the kiss she's wordlessly asking for.

She moans softly, melting against me. I don't even mind when she takes her hands off the glass and grips my shoulders. The Olivia I came home to was pissed off—and I'll find out why, later. But this Olivia is the happy, playful girl, the real version of her.

"I love you, Sir," she whispers.

"I love you, too." I shove down my sweats enough to free my cock, and move Olivia so she's standing over the back of the couch. Then I touch the glistening folds of her pussy. She's practically dripping with her arousal, and I can't wait to feel her clamping hard on my dick. I thrust into her without warning. Her gasp transforms into a wanton moan. It won't take her long to come, and I want to be right there with her. I bring my hand around to choke her, because I love the control in that move, the way she submits in her trust. She knows I'll never let anything happen to her, even when I can control her very breath.

The chain of her collar is frail against my palm, so I brush it aside. As I do, her pendant swings around.

There's more writing there, in addition to the *Babydoll* Jaxon originally had engraved.

I go still in her pussy and hold her hips against the couch with mine, ignoring her attempts to push back on my cock. "What's this?"

"What's what?" she asks, breathlessly.

"Your collar," I say, sliding it around the chain so I can see the pendant better.

A burst of savage pride fills me at the sight of the new engraving. Above the word *Babydoll* on the lower half of the circle are three new words.

"Fuck, that's beautiful," I say.

She turns slightly and gives me a sly look. "I had it done the other day. I wondered when you'd notice."

I spin the necklace around so the pendant dangles between her shoulder blades, the words facing out. Then I hold her hips with one hand and reach for her clit with my other, rubbing the sensitive, slippery nub until Olivia cries out with pleasure. I empty into her with a roar, my vision blurring with emotion at the sight of those words —words she wears with her everywhere she goes because she never takes this necklace off.

Jaxon's and Ryder's Babydoll.

Jaxon and I are the luckiest fucking assholes in the whole goddamn world.

8

Jaxon

On Sunday night, Ryder's working late and I'm at the penthouse with Olivia. We're watching TV and she's sitting between my legs, both of us facing the television. I absently toy with her daytime collar, lifting the chain up and down so the pendant slides back and forth, flashing the new engraving she put there. *Jaxon's and Ryder's Babydoll*. When I came home the other night, she and Ryder had just finished fucking, and Ryder proudly pointed to her necklace.

Something had swelled bigger in my chest at the sight of it, at the sight of her having claimed us so explicitly. Both of us.

While I mess with her necklace, she doesn't complain even though I've got to be blocking her view of the TV with every slide of the pendant. I bury my face in her hair and inhale her sweetness.

Even though I know our problems are far from over,

what with Daniel skulking around and stalking Olivia, this is a moment of peace, right here, right now. Our new hire, Lin Rosewood, is on it, spending the bulk of her days reviewing everything we can find about Daniel Pinoir.

And just like that, with that fucker's name flitting through my head, the contentment I'd been feeling evaporates.

As if sensing my change in mood, Olivia places her hand on my knee and strokes her fingernails over the fabric of my jeans.

"Are you trying to ask me for something, Babydoll?" I say.

"Maybe," she says slowly.

I splay my hand over her lower stomach and dip my fingers beneath the waistband of her pajama pants. But suddenly, she sits up.

"What?" I say. "What is it?"

She points at the television. "Gah, my mother. She is *everywhere*, I swear."

It looks as if the congresswoman is giving a speech of some kind, or, no, she's taking questions from a group of people in a crowded room. *Town Hall Meeting with Congresswoman Blankenship in Forest Hills.*

"She wanted me to attend that stupid thing," Olivia says.

"Really? Why?"

"Optics," she says. "Ugh, I'm getting mad just thinking about it."

"Well, that's easily fixed," I say, reaching for the remote.

Just as I'm about to change the channel, though, the

camera view switches to the steps outside of the town hall. Protesters line the steps, holding large signs. Their faces display anger and resentment, bitterness, rage.

The signs read *Frak the Foxes* and *Jobs Over Animals*. People are shouting an indecipherable chant. And standing with everyone, holding one of those signs and chanting, is a vaguely familiar face.

"Where do I know her from?" I murmur.

"Who?" Olivia asks.

"That woman right there," I say, pointing at the screen, but the camera angle switches again. "Fuck, hang on. I need to find this."

I bring up the station's channel on my phone and wait impatiently for it to load. Too many damned advertisements.

But then the camera angle on the TV switches back to the familiar woman.

"Aha," I say, and snap a picture of the TV screen. I can get a clearer image later from the video when the station uploads it to their site, but this will do for now. I study the somewhat-blurry face and enlarge it, then hold it up to Olivia, who is staring at me over her shoulder while wearing a bemused expression. "Do you know her?"

Olivia's eyebrows shoot up in surprise. "Holy shit...I think that's the bodyguard who hassled me about Ryder and you. Remember?"

"Oh yeah, I remember," I growl.

"Why are you so mad? You guys kicked her out. It's just a weird coincidence," she says.

I shake my head. In the security business, there are no such things as coincidences.

Ryder

I close the file sent to me by Lin, and lean back in my desk. We're nowhere near finding a connection between Daniel Pinoir and Kinasey County. It's just not there. After opening our inter-office messaging system, I send Lin a missive. *What about Genevieve Warren? Any connections there?*

I know the answer will be no, because I've been monitoring Genevieve's movements since the gala. She's back in London and was photographed at a recent museum opening, holding hands with an older man. Maybe she's moved on. I sure as fuck hope so. Her posts on social media all show her thoughtfully looking into the distance, with captions like #WorkingOnMySelf and #PersonalInsights. I don't trust any of it, but it's my job not to trust it.

At any rate, Lin and most of our other daytime crew have all gone home, so I'll hear from her with an answer tomorrow.

My phone buzzes on the desk, the screen lighting up to tell me Jaxon is calling.

"What is it?" I answer.

"You need to work on your phone etiquette," he says.

"Is that why you called? So we can practice?"

He sighs. "Don't be a dick."

"Too late."

"I'm sending you a picture and I want your gut impression."

It doesn't sound like he's sending me a pic of Olivia,

but I hold out hope until the photo pops up on my screen. "What the hell is this?" I ask.

"A protest. Just look at it, tell me what you think."

I peer at the shot for a moment, and then I see why he's sending it to me. It's the briefest glimpse, in the foreground, of a trio of people wearing all black. I almost mistake them for security before I realize one of them is holding a sign and they're part of the protest. The one with the sign is a blond-haired woman with a lean but muscular frame. She's tall, capable-looking.

I say, "That's the woman we fired for confronting Olivia when she was supposed to be guarding her."

That confrontation had led to the bodyguard's dismissal, and Olivia had overheard everything and thought I was getting rid of *her*. My chest clenches at the memory of everything that came after—Olivia's kidnapping, and the fear and panic that had overtaken both me and Jaxon as a result, until we found her.

"Yeah, it's the same woman," Jaxon says.

"Lisa A…" I can't remember her last name.

"Albertson," he says.

"And where is this?" I ask, then I see the caption at the bottom of the screen. *Town Hall Meeting with Congresswoman Blankenship in Forest Hills.*

"Forest Hills," I say. "Shit. Jax, Forest Hills is in Kinasey County."

"Too many fucking coincidences," he says, then hangs up.

I stare around my office, feeling like the building has tilted slightly with this new information. There's no such thing as a coincidence in this business. If Lisa Albertson is at a protest involving Olivia's mother, then we need to fucking pay attention.

A couple seconds later, a text comes through from Jaxon. *Let Lin know we want to talk to her and the rest of the investigations team, first thing tomorrow.*

On it, I type back.

We're going to figure this the fuck out and end this nonsense once and for all.

Olivia

I can only stare at Jaxon after he gets off the phone with Ryder. Then I find my voice. "*More* coincidences?"

"Kinasey County," he says, then points to the screen. "That's what's happening up there. Your mom's environmental work."

"Oh wow, yeah. That's why it sounded so familiar. She's always talking about those black-eared foxes in Kinasey County." I bury my face in my hands, struggling to think. "So...Daniel isn't a part of this. Not if it has to do with politics."

Jaxon chuckles. "Oh, he could still be part of it. Don't rule out a perfect storm, sweetheart."

I shoot him a look. "You sounded super patronizing right there. Watch it, mister."

"I *am* your daddy," he says, grinning.

"Maybe *I* want to be the daddy," I say.

"Sure," he says, laughing. "Wrestle me for the privilege." He leans back against the couch cushion.

I know we should be freaking out, worrying about

Kinasey County and foxes and fires and stalkers. But right now, seeing that smug smile on Jaxon's face and knowing he's challenging me for the right to be in charge, well...all it does is make me want to win.

With a loud battle cry, I leap across the sofa cushions and land on him.

I don't have a freaking chance. His hands band around my arms and he lifts me up before flipping us over so he's on top. He holds both of my wrists with one of his hands and dips his face to my neck. His beard tickles my skin, and then there's a sharp bite of his teeth on my throat.

"Hey!" I yell.

He pulls away from me and grins. "Who's your daddy?"

Laughing, I try to pull away and say, "You are such a dork—"

He steals my words and my breath in a kiss, and then I'm moaning all kinds of nonsense about how he's my daddy and I'll do anything he wants, if he'll just put his dick in me and make me come already, because something about this rough, bossy, dominant man just does it for me every time, making me wet and needy. The hard length of him presses against my hip.

"Please, Daddy," I whisper.

His kiss is hard, insistent, his tongue forcing its way in and commanding me to yield.

My phone rings, and Jaxon pulls away slightly.

"Come back," I say, trying to hold him in place by wrapping my leg around his.

Chuckling, he picks up my phone and hands it to me.

"Noooo, it's my mom," I say. "Argh."

"This is good," he says, sitting up and pulling me with him. "We should ask her about the laws she wants to pass and what the story is up there."

It's worse than a cold shower, and I shiver. Jaxon wraps his arm around my shoulders as I answer my phone.

"Hey, Mom."

"Olivia, I heard a few things at the town hall meeting. The people there are in an uproar—"

"I saw footage on the news," I say.

"This thing with the black-eared foxes has a lot of people upset. Someone mentioned that I should be feeling the 'heat' of their disapproval."

It takes a second for her words to sink in. "Heat," I say slowly, "as in fire?"

"Yes." She takes a deep breath. "I know your boyfriends are in security, and they're taking good care of you, I'm sure, other than, of course, the day of the fire—"

"That wasn't their fault," I'm quick to say. "It wasn't even the bodyguards' faults. No one could have imagined it would get so out of hand. I mean, tranquilizer darts?"

"Exactly," she says. "So I'm offering to hire extra security for you. Mr. Marsel and Mr. Callihan are welcome to pull them from their own team, but I want you with four guards instead of two—"

"Out of the question," I say.

"What? Why?" she asks.

"I'm not going about my life with four people shadowing every move I make."

Her voice is cold as she says, "With your current relationship shenanigans, I didn't think you'd notice a crowd."

Anger flashes, heating my cheeks and making my throat pound. I don't even stop to think of a retort; I hang up.

Jaxon cocks his head at me in curiosity, but I'm so livid, I can't speak.

My mom calls back immediately. I don't pick up. A couple of seconds later, she texts.

I'm sorry for saying that. It wasn't fair of me to do so. I'm just very worried about you, Olivia.

Frowning at the phone, I compose my answer in my head before I start typing, because I'm not sure whether I'm going to respond at all. Then I write, *I accept your apology, but I'm not ready to talk now. I'll let Jaxon and Ryder know about your idea, but I'll also let them know I disagree with it.*

Thank you, she writes back. *Please call me when you're ready to talk.*

I look over at Jaxon, surprised. Other than my mom's initial mean comment, this is one of the most adult, communicative interactions I've ever had with my mother. When I recount the conversation to him, he grabs me in his arms and inhales deeply, his face pressed to my neck.

"You know I'd give you extra bodyguards in a heartbeat if you'd let me," he says.

"I know," I say, holding tightly to his shoulders.

"It kills me to think you're in danger," he says.

"I'm being careful, now."

"Good." He peels up my shirt, exposing my bra-clad breasts. Bringing his head back down, he sucks one into his mouth, so hard that I hiss in pain even while my pussy clenches in desire. His movements are fast and rough as he removes my pants and panties, barely taking the time to shove down his own pants far enough to free his cock which is hot and thick and pressing into me, filling me, claiming me.

"You're so precious to me," he says, stroking slowly, lazily, at complete odds with his rush to get me naked. "We're going to take care of you, Babydoll."

His movements are slow and he builds me up gradually, his voice in my ear is rough and low as he grunts all kinds of nonsensical praise about what a good girl I am, how he could die with me and be happy, how he needs me all the time, how he wants to take care of me forever.

We come at almost the exact same time, holding tight to each other. Jaxon crashes his mouth against mine. I pour my feelings into the kiss, trying to show him with my lips and tongue what my heart is feeling. Love.

This is the best place to be—surrounded by, possessed by Jaxon.

I look deeply into his eyes in just the way he likes me to, and I see the truth there. He means every word. They're going to take care of me.

9

Jaxon

The tech room at Ironwood is full of the whirring of computers and the scent of machines and ink. This is the thinking part of our company. Right now, it's a small operation, but the room is big and one of these days we're going to have the manpower to rival that of a small city's police department.

A wide table sits in the middle of the room, surrounded by folding chairs. Ryder and I, along with Lin and Leonie, sit at one end, a pile of folders and photographs between us. Off to the side is a glass board with lines and photos, straight out of a police procedural TV drama, with a picture of Daniel Pinoir on one side, and a large company logo on the other. JTS.

"Talk to me about this," I say to Lin and Leonie, pointing to the JTS logo. "What is that?"

"JTS is our other suspect in the fire," Leonie says,

impatiently flipping her long, gray braid over one shoulder.

"Cool," Ryder says. "Why?"

"It's JonBell Tech Solutions, a company with a vested interest in continuing the fracking going on in Kinase County," Lin adds.

"And the fracking is what Congresswoman Blankenship wants to stop?" Ryder asks.

"Exactly," Lin says.

I'm slowly putting things together. There's a reason I hire people to investigate—investigation is not my strength. I've always been the muscles and the business instincts, not the brains. "So JTS comes after the congresswoman, and her daughter, in an attempt to, what, scare her off?"

"It's an intimidation tactic," Lin says.

"And this is more plausible than Olivia's ex coming after her after escaping jail?" Ryder asks, sounding doubtful.

I want to point out that Daniel actually saved Olivia from the fire, but the argument is weak even to my mind. I believe Olivia believes she saw Daniel. Hell, a part of me even believes he was really there and really saved her. But he still could've started the damned fire to begin with.

It's the tranquilizer darts that give credence to the JTS idea Lin and Leonie are putting forth. Tranquilizer darts, taking out witnesses and security guards before grabbing Olivia—that's not Daniel's MO. He's more the kind of asshole to skulk around in the shadows and wait for the right opportunity.

"Tell us more about JonBell Tech," I say, trying not to

growl out the words and pound on the table and throw things, like I really want to do.

Leonie and Lin go through everything they have on JTS. The corporation makes its money from digging into the earth for natural gas—fracking—and that, in turn, is disrupting the habitat of the black-eared fox. And even though the black-eared fox isn't yet endangered, it is considered "vulnerable," which is one step down from endangered.

Leonie pulls an image of the black-eared fox up on the large monitor.

"It's cute," Ryder says derisively. "Looks like it would be the perfect thing for a politician to champion so she can look better."

Lin gives him a dirty look. I know it's his defensiveness of Olivia talking, but he's also not wrong. How often do slimy amphibians get the kind of bleeding-heart attention Faye Blankenship is giving to this fox?

"Anyway," Leonie says, "that brings us to what we need from you two."

"What's that?" I ask.

"Do you want us to put more attention on Daniel Pinoir, or on JonBell Tech Solutions?" she asks. "We can investigate both at the same time, but not well. I'm thinking we put five of our people on one, and leave two others to keep looking into the other."

It's a great point. "My gut's telling me that JTS is the culprit here," I say, "but Pinoir is a real threat. I want to know what he was doing there. And if the tracker is associated with Kinasey County, and JTS, then how he found Olivia. Seems unlikely our guys would've missed a tail on the way there with Olivia."

"JTS, then," Ryder says, nodding with finality. "Put most of your focus there, and choose two people to keep an eye on Pinoir."

"Gotcha," Lin says.

Ryder and I get up to go, and I cast one final look at Daniel Pinoir's mugshot. In it, he stares sullenly at the photographer as if daring them to start a fight with him.

I'd fight that asshole, and I'd win. I'd make him so fucking sorry for ever hurting Olivia.

∾

Olivia

I'm wearing my most professional-looking outfit—the very same clothes I wore when I gave my final project presentation, in fact. Pencil skirt, silk shirt, heels. The chair I'm perched on isn't very comfortable, and I shift this way and that. My ass is a little sore from a spanking Ryder gave me last night. When I'd protested the treatment because I hadn't done anything wrong, he'd smiled and said I was getting spanked "just because I fucking feel like it, okay, princess?"

And I said okay. Because the spanking got me wet, and Jaxon watching the whole thing got me wet, and the sex was fantastic.

I'm completely addicted to these men. I'm trying to trust that there's no end to our relationship, but I keep waiting for the rug to get pulled out from under me. Or maybe I'll wake up from this incredible dream...I hate to think of it.

Reminding myself of the job at hand, I read over the

rubric in front of me while I wait for my first interviewee to show up at the warehouse. No, this isn't the most comfortable place to conduct interviews, but I don't have an office, and I don't want the distractions we'd encounter at a coffee shop. Jaxon and Ryder offered a me space at Ironwood, but I think that would be even more intimidating to the potential hires, having to run through a gamut of beefy bodyguards just to talk to little old me. Bad enough that Terrence and Squid are hulking off to the side of the warehouse, ready to spring to my defense.

The first interviewee, Kathryn Feldsworth, comes in, peering uncertainly into the large warehouse. We chat for a long time. I like her, and along with everyone else coming in for an interview today, she passed all the background checks Ryder insisted on running. Of course, Ryder emphasized the fact that nearly everything can be faked these days, so I still need to be smart.

Because apparently we're no longer worried only about Daniel; we're also worried about JonBell Tech Solutions.

Shaking off the thought, I return to the matter at hand—finding at least two people who can help me get Youth Arts off the ground.

Once we're finished with the interview, I shake Kathryn's hand, then jot a few notes on the rubric in front of me. There's nothing in the rubric about "gut feeling," so I add a place for that at the very bottom and give her the highest score possible. I have a good feeling about her. Then, just as quickly, I scribble out that additional score. I don't want "gut feeling" to be an excuse for subconscious biases in the workplace. What if I think I don't like someone just because they look different than I do?

The next woman is also quite agreeable, but as we talk, it becomes clear to me that although she is passionate about art, she doesn't like kids. When I ask her how she would handle a rowdy group of high school freshmen, she gets a look of horror on her face.

It's a bummer to give her glowing scores on the rubric except in the one element that matters most to the organization: working with youth.

I interview a couple of other promising candidates. Other than the woman who didn't like kids, I want to hire everyone. I'm going to hate contacting those who didn't make the cut.

Getting up, I give a good stretch and try to walk off the ache in my ass. I'm just sitting down when the last interviewee enters the warehouse. He looks vaguely familiar, and I'm trying to figure out if he was in one of my classes at San Esteban School of the Arts. I shove the rubric aside and scan his application, which I'd printed out for the interview, to see if SESA is written anywhere on it, but I don't see it. I give him another look.

He pauses and squints at me before sitting down.

"Wait a minute," he says, tapping his chin. "I know you from somewhere..."

"Oh," I say, laughing a little as I recognize his eyebrow ring. "It's you! From Artisanal Brew."

When he cocks his head in question, his eyebrow ring glints in the overhead lights. "Arisanal Brew..."

"The café," I say. "You tripped over my extra chair. I replaced your coffee for your boss."

"Oh! Right." He smacks himself on the forehead and

grins. "I'm so glad you remembered, because it would've driven me crazy to not be sure where I knew you from."

"I thought maybe you went to SESA, like me."

"Nope." He shrugs. "No formal art training. But I do have a background in education."

"Excellent," I say. "Let's talk about that first, then. Wait a minute...if you're here, does that mean you got fired over the coffee thing?"

"No, no, nothing like that," he says. "Although I'm sure it didn't help. No, I'm still employed, but being afraid of my boss day in, day out is getting exhausting."

"Yeah, I bet," I say, trying to sympathize although I have only volunteered, never worked for a paycheck. "Anyway, I'm Olivia Santiago."

"Nate Boyd," he says, shaking my hand.

We go through the interview questions, and I like Nate's responses. Unfortunately, my bodily response to him is one of aversion. I don't like being close to the guy, and I can't really articulate why. He would fail the "gut feeling" rubric, but there's a reason I scratched that off of my scoring system. I could just not like him because he asked me out and I feel awkward, and that's hardly a reason to keep someone out of a job. It's not his fault I already have not one, but two boyfriends.

Nate shakes my hand at the end of the interview. He even gives a friendly wave to Terrence and Squid. Everyone else gave the bodyguards a scared look, but Nate is just overall bubbly and friendly. He'd be a good asset to the organization, and I can already tell by looking at the rubric, he scored higher than everyone except Kathryn, the first woman I interviewed.

Terrence and Squid look relieved to get out of here.

It's probably boring standing around when nothing is happening. Not for the first time, I feel bad for having bodyguards. But it's a job and they're getting paid, so I'm trying to let that go.

"Are you guys ready?" I ask, then wince inwardly. Of course they're ready.

Terrence goes outside first, checking things out, I guess, and then he waves that it's safe for Squid to bring me through the warehouse door. They wait while I set the alarm and lock up.

Once I'm back at the penthouse, I strip out of my professional clothes and put on sweatpants and one of Ryder's t-shirts. It smells like pine trees and I just want to rub my face in it. Wearing it is nearly as good as that. I gather my papers and notes from the interviews and go into the living room, where I hug a throw pillow that holds Jaxon's citrus scent.

Surrounded by my guys in scent if not in person, I look over the score sheets. I want to do this in the fairest, most logical way possible, so I fold over the tops of each page, obscuring the applicants' names, although I first set aside the rubric score sheet for the woman who doesn't like children. That's just not going to work.

Once the names are all hidden, I add up the different scores. I'm going to start with two hires, and the two with the highest scores will be the ones I offer positions to first.

When I straighten the paper on top, I'm not surprised to see Kathryn Feldsworth's name. I immediately look up her phone number and give her a call.

"After talking with me today, are you still interested in the position?" I ask her.

"Oh, yes!" she says.

We talk out start dates and salary, and I answer a few questions she thought of after the interview. She is effusive and enthusiastic, and I'm smiling while I get off the phone.

When I unfold the top of the second paper, I'm relieved that it isn't Nate Boyd. But when I give the applicant a call, she turns me down, citing a reluctance to work in the Bellefleur District. She thanks me for the opportunity. Once I hang up, I sigh in annoyance. But no matter—there are still a handful of perfectly acceptable potential hires.

I straighten out the third paper to reveal Nate Boyd's name.

Of course.

I'm tempted to toss the paper aside, but the whole reason for the rubric is so I can make logical decisions which aren't tainted by bias. So, I give him a call.

"Hello?" he answers.

"Hi, Nate? This is Olivia Santiago, from Youth Arts."

"Oh, hey," he says, and I hear a smile in his voice.

"I have good news, and good news," I say.

"Don't tease me," he says. "Did I pass inspection? Do I get the job?"

"You do," I say, shoving aside my misgivings. "When can you start?"

I chat with him like I did with Kathryn, and my impulse to take it all back disintegrates. He's a nice guy, and he's not acting at all weird that he tried to pick me up. This is going to work out, I think.

By the time Nate and I get off the phone, I'm full of excitement. I can't wait to tell Jaxon and Ryder about my day's progress. When I start to text them, though, a new text pops up from my mother.

I'm going to be in San Esteban for lunch tomorrow, and I've made us a reservation at Chez Michel for 12:30. I hope you'll join me and we can finally talk.

Fuck it. I've been skating around this confrontation for far too long. Heaving a deep breath, I text back, *I'll be there.*

10

Olivia

C hez Michel is the kind of restaurant a politician like Faye Blankenship wants to be seen in. It's not too terribly fancy, but it's fancy enough that the other patrons aren't going to hassle her. The chances of running into rich donors who support her cause are fairly high, so she can look sociable while she shakes their hands, but she can also excuse herself quickly because she's enjoying a "quiet lunch" with her daughter.

Her daughter being me, of course.

I've been eating at restaurants like Chez Michel since my mother entered the political arena ten years ago. Something about sitting here in front of her makes me feel twelve years old again, unsure of my posture after Mom's repeated attempts to get me to sit up straight, "but not so straight you look like you're thrusting your chest out." Because I was an early bloomer, the whole "sticking your chest out" thing hit me especially hard. Girls were jealous, boys teased.

Added to being an early bloomer, my mother's face was suddenly in the news as a major contender for Congress, and random people talking to me about whether that was a good thing or a bad thing, and life was miserable.

I do not miss being a pre-teen.

Still, we always had enough to eat. I was healthy, if not always happy. I was loved, even though I was lonely.

"Olivia," Mom says gently, and I bring my attention back to her instead of the tablecloth where I'd been blankly staring. "How are you? Truly? The fire was horrific, and I wanted to be there for you, but..."

She trails off.

"But there was a media circus, I get it," I say, and I'm proud of myself for not sounding like a sullen teenager. "I understand, truly."

"Thank you," she says. "But my question remains: how are you?"

I decide not to tell her about the nightmare that woke me up last night, when Ryder held me tight to his chest and reminded me over and over again that I was safe. It had taken a solid fifteen minutes of breathing in his evergreen scent before I could relax enough to fall back asleep, held in the protection of his arms.

"I'm all right," I say. "I get flashes of what happened, and it makes me panic sometimes, but it's always pretty brief."

She nods. "That makes sense. And otherwise? How is your organization going?"

I fill her in on my recent hires, on the warehouse, and

all of the other plans I have. By the time I'm through, our food is nearly gone from our plates and I realize that as much as I thought this would be like previous lunch dates where my mother's focus was on everything except me, she's actually paying attention to everything I'm saying. I wonder what's changed for her.

"Dessert?" our server asks, brandishing a smaller version of their menu.

"Let's have a look, shall we?" Mom asks me, and I realize that yes, everything is different.

Then again, she hasn't yet brought up my relationship with Jaxon and Ryder, so the dessert might be a way to keep me here long enough for her to do that.

Sure enough, after we've received our crème brûlée and coffee, she folds her hands in front of her and says, "I'd really like to talk to you about the two men in your life."

Yep, there it is. "Sure," I say slowly. "What do you want to discuss?"

"It doesn't seem like it's a passing fancy," she says. "I've seen them more than once now when you're in danger, and each time, they've been completely torn up. I thought Jaxon was going to drag me out of the ambulance after your gala, so he could ride with you to the hospital instead of me."

"You rode with me to the hospital?" I ask, for some reason fixating on that.

"Of course," she says.

I'm quiet for a moment, thinking about that, and why it surprises me. I know my mother loves me, but since I ignored her wishes and went for an art degree instead of something "practical," there's been a rift between us. It's been hard to remember that she has feelings—she's been so cold.

"Talk to me, Olivia," she says gently.

"I've just missed you," I say, my eyes filling with tears that I quickly blink away.

Her eyes get shiny with tears, too. "I'm sorry I haven't been here for you. Or rather, that I've been...judgmental. I did some research after we last talked, about polyamory and nontraditional relationships. In the end, I just want you to be happy, sweetheart. If your two men make you happy, if they are good to you and treasure you like you are meant to be treasured, then I will support you, no matter what."

"Even if the media catches wind of the relationship?" I ask.

"Even then," she says. "*Love is love* is completely a part of my beliefs, and that will apply to all forms of love between consenting adults, no matter their genders or number."

"They treat me very well," I say.

She frowns at me. "I hear a *but* in there."

"It's not them," I say, "it's me. I'm having a hard time believing that they want to keep me around forever, even though they're saying it's true."

Sighing a little, she smiles at squeezes my hand. "Being in a relationship, any relationship, requires vulnerability and a leap of faith. I'm guessing a relationship with two men would require even more vulnerability than usual. There are two people to maneuver around, two hearts, in addition to your own, that require care and tenderness."

"You're right," I say, looking at her kind smile and

feeling my shoulders ease. "That's exactly it. I worry about disappointing one, and losing both."

"I don't think that could happen," she says, "but of course I don't know them very well. Maybe if you brought them over sometime for a nice family dinner, that could change?"

I can't help the grin forming on my face. "Yeah, I think I can do that."

Our conversation veers toward more practical things, like her work in Kinasey County. After speaking with Jaxon the other day, Mom has local law enforcement investigating JTS and the company's attack on her home, and on us. It's just a suspicion at this point, and there's no strong evidence tying the company to the fire. But at least someone else knows about it, so Ironwood Security isn't doing all the work on their own.

At the end of the meal, she gives me a tight hug good-bye, squeezing me hard. When she pulls back, she dabs at her eyes again. "I've missed you, Olivia."

"I've missed you, too," I say sincerely.

As my bodyguards take me back to the penthouse, I reflect on the lunch date with my mother. I never thought that she, of all people, would give me excellent relationship advice. Especially when that relationship is far from the standard.

Now I need to talk to Jaxon and Ryder. It's time to be vulnerable—not only naked with my body, but naked with my heart and my emotions.

Jaxon

The elevator doors open into my penthouse, and I freeze with surprise. Olivia is kneeling on the floor, head bowed, completely naked. It's a classic submissive pose, something most subs have to be trained to do. Did she look it up online or something?

She's wearing nothing except her *Babydoll* necklace. Her knees are apart and from a different angle, I'll be able to see all of her pussy. She looks delicious, but I want to wrap her up in a blanket and cuddle her. No, maybe I want to fuck her first. I can't decide what I want to do, except *everything*.

"Babydoll?" I ask, striding forward.

She lifts her head slightly and looks up at me. "Daddy," she says with a small smile. "I'm waiting for you and Mr. Ryder."

"How long have you been waiting?"

"Not long, I don't think," she says. "It's peaceful. I want to talk to you both."

I cup her cheek and say, "Well, he's on his way. He was powering things down for the night when I left Ironwood."

She leans into my touch and sighs. "I love you, Jaxon."

"I love you too, Olivia."

This behavior of hers is different, but it's not concerning, just strange. I'm about to ask if she wants to stand up for a hug when the elevator doors whoosh open and Ryder steps into the penthouse.

"Oh, we're playing already, huh?" he says, dropping his keys, wallet, and phone on the table next to the door.

"I'm not playing yet," Olivia says, looking up at him

through her eyelashes. Her beautiful gray eyes are wide and serious. "I want to have a conversation."

Ryder nods. "Okay, then."

Bending down, I kiss the crown of her head. "What's up, Olivia?"

"I'm here to be vulnerable with you," she says, her voice soft, like she's afraid of saying the words.

Suddenly I get it, although Ryder still looks a little puzzled. I sit down on the floor in front of her and take one of her hands. Although he's slower on the uptake, Ryder joins us, taking Olivia's other hand.

Her breathing is fast; she's nervous. I pull my gaze away from her heaving chest, because even now, her tits are turning me on. *Focus, Jaxon. Be the daddy she needs you to be.*

"We're ready for whatever you want to tell us," I say.

She nods and looks at each of us in turn. Taking a deep breath, she says, "Sometimes I use being submissive as an excuse to be passive. It isn't on purpose, I don't think—it's just the way I'm wired, you know? But I have things that I want very much, and I'm afraid to tell you both because I don't want to lose you."

"You could never lose us," I say.

"It's a fear just the same. My stepfather walked out after I'd completely bonded with him, and then my mother became a politician, and I've felt abandoned at times, even though"—she chuckles in a self-deprecating way—"I've lived an incredibly privileged life. I recognize that. But I still worry. No, it's not worry. It's terror. I'm so afraid, you guys, that if you knew how much...how much..." She breaks off, her shoulders shaking.

I tug on her hand.

"No, don't comfort me right now," she says. "I need to finish this."

I want to gather her in my arms and I can tell Ryder wants to do the same thing. He and I look helplessly at each other before turning back to Olivia.

After a long moment, she continues speaking. "I love you so much," she says. "And sometimes I worry that the strength of that love will be the very thing to drive you away. That it's too fierce, too much, and you won't like it. As a submissive, I should accept what you give and be grateful, right?"

"That's not how it works, Babydoll," I say.

"Well, it's how I feel," she says. "Even though I'm a submissive, my love is dominant."

Fuck, that's beautiful. This girl takes my breath away —not just with her beauty, but with her mind, with her words.

"Your love is perfect, however you want to show it," I tell her. "Fierce, passive, whatever you're feeling, that's right for us."

"Sometimes it's messy," she says.

"I've told you. I like messy," I say.

Ryder nods. "We fucking *love* messy, baby girl. And I don't know how we can convince you, truly show you that we are in this forever. But we are."

"Look," I say, "Ryder and I have talked. In the interest of being vulnerable, I want you to know that we want to marry you. When we say forever, we mean it. And I love you—forever."

Ryder takes her hand and presses her palm to his lips. "I love you forever, too, Olivia. You're our babydoll and it isn't just a passing kink or a phase for us. Our dominant love can handle your dominant love, trust me."

She looks between us both, her eyes filling with tears. "You can't both marry me."

"Not legally," Ryder says, "but we can wrap up our assets and everything else legally, and do a commitment ceremony. Or you can marry one of us legally. I don't mind if it's Jax instead of me—"

"And I wouldn't mind if you pick Ryder for that," I'm quick to add.

"I could never choose between the two of you," she says.

"Then we'll exchange rings," I say, "and have a party. However you want to do it."

She squeezes her eyes shut and takes a deep breath before opening them again and peering at me. "I'm not ready to be engaged."

"We haven't proposed yet," Ryder says with a wink.

"Good," she says, laughing.

"But it'll happen," I say. "Don't doubt it, Babydoll."

"I know, Daddy." She turns those huge gray eyes on me and smiles so big, my whole body lights up in happiness, just at the sight of her.

"Are you satisfied?" I ask. "Is there anything else you want to talk to us about?"

She shakes her head. "That's everything." Then she winks. "I don't know that I could say I'm 'satisfied,' though."

I get to my feet and rest my hand on the top of her head. "Excellent."

"There's something important we need to talk about,

Babydoll," Ryder says, also standing. "And it's just between you and me."

"I don't want to leave Jaxon out—"

"No, he can stay," Ryder says, meeting my gaze.

I'm curious what he has in mind that has him so worked up. This should be interesting.

Ryder continues, "Jaxon can stay, but this is a matter for the two of us to resolve—you and me, Babydoll."

11

Olivia

Jaxon moves aside, and I'm left kneeling on the floor in front of Ryder. He looks down at me, his blue eyes glittering with intensity.

"Hey, Babydoll," he says, his voice rough.

"Hi, Mr. Ryder," I whisper.

His gaze darkens, that bright blue twisting into something full of sweet, painful promise. My pussy is already wet, but this look of his has me anticipating what's to come, and you know what will be coming? Me.

"Get on all fours," he says.

I'm quick to comply. Even though I know whatever punishments he has in store will be delightful, I'm not eager to tempt him to start early.

He stares directly at my face and his mouth turns up at the corner as he says, "Beg for Jaxon's cock."

Turning my head slightly so I can see Jaxon, I say, "Please, Daddy, give me your cock?"

Jaxon doesn't respond. His dick is hard; I can see the outline through his work slacks. But despite that, and the hungry expression in his brown eyes, he doesn't make a move toward me.

"Please, Daddy," I say. "Please give me your cock. I need it."

Ryder makes a tsking sound and rests his hand on the crown of my head. His palm is heavy and warm. "It's not working, little girl. That's too bad."

"Please, please," I say to Jaxon, infusing as much need and desire into my expression as I can.

Jaxon merely shakes his head. He's on Ryder's side, which just sucks for me, I guess. Whatever has upset Ryder, Jaxon will support him.

"It's not going to work," Ryder says, "but I love to hear you beg. Keep going, little one, and I'll be right back."

"Daddy, please," I say, begging Jaxon loudly enough to make Ryder happy.

His handsome, bearded face remains impassive.

I make him all kinds of promises, how I'll be a good girl for him, how I'll make him feel amazing, how he can do whatever he wants with his cock if he'll just please, please give it to me.

Jaxon smirks and folds his arms across his chest. He looks handsome and untouchable as ever.

Ryder's footsteps get louder as he returns to the living room.

I scowl at Jaxon. "Come on," I whine. "This isn't fair."

Ryder's swat on my ass is sharp, and I gasp.

"Ow, why'd you do that?" I ask.

"Sounds to me like you're giving Jaxon some attitude."

"Sorry, Sir," I whisper, and then to Jaxon, I add, "Sorry, Daddy."

Ryder spanks me again, and I jerk forward on my hands and knees.

"Hold still, Babydoll," he growls, then nudges something forward on the floor next to me.

"Yes, Sir." I look to the side and see a glass bowl full of ice and water. And sitting in that water is a butt plug and nipple clamps. Oh, shit. That's going to be uncomfortable. "Um, Mr. Ryder, Sir? I don't think—"

"That's enough talking, Olivia," he says.

"But I need to—"

"You have a safe word." His voice is stern, but amused.

He thinks my discomfort is *amusing*? Irate, I look over at Jaxon. Surely he'll put a stop to this nonsense. But no, his cock looks even harder, if possible, and he simply watches, his dark eyes full of interest.

This is unfair. Huffing a breath, I say, "Well, I have something to say—"

He grabs my hair and pulls my head back. Gently—it doesn't hurt in the slightest—but I won't be able to wiggle away from his dominating gaze. He says, "You will be punished because I say so."

"But what did I do?"

His voice is quiet and low. "You'll find out. The next word out of your mouth better be your safe word, or you're going to be very sorry, little princess."

My pussy gets even wetter. Ryder lets go of my hair and slides his hand down my spine. From the corner of my gaze, I examine the bowl of ice water. The plug is resting on the bottom, because it's metal. Same with the nipple clamps.

The snap of a bottle of lube opening is similar to the sound of a spank, and I flinch.

Ryder chuckles. "You're so beautiful, Babydoll. You'll take your punishment like a good, obedient girl, and you and I are going to have a little chat, and then all three of us are going to have a very good time."

I bite my lip to keep from saying anything.

He slides his finger over my crack, spreading the lube around before he concentrates on my anus. I try not to squirm at the intrusion of his finger, because it doesn't matter how many times Ryder and Jaxon play with my ass, I'm always left a little uncomfortable at the taboo aspect of it.

Yet they make it feel so damn good, every single time.

Everything's slippery back there, and then Ryder's other hand comes into view. He takes the butt plug from the bowl of ice water.

My body tenses up. Not with fear, but with the expectation of discomfort, and the anticipation of pleasure. I'll take a lot of punishment because I love these men and I know they'll both make it worthwhile in the end. They always do. Pain morphs into pleasure and back again in an endless cycle of ecstasy, and I am hooked.

"Oh yeah, that's nice and cold," Ryder says, then touches the plug to one of my ass cheeks.

Goosebumps erupt over my skin at the cold sensation. I want to tell him not to do it, but the truth is, I want to give him my submission. My discomfort, too, if it will give him satisfaction.

He fits the plug against my hole and presses it into me. It's so cold, it feels as if it's burning. I groan and try to scoot forward, out of his reach, but he chuckles darkly and grabs my hips, holding me in place.

"So beautiful," he says once the plug is in. "You're magnificent."

Tears spring to my eyes. The plug feels weird and cold and foreign, and yet Ryder places a warm, loving kiss at the base of my spine, and I know I'm treasured, adored.

"Up you go," he says, pulling on my shoulders. "On your knees."

Fuck. Those nipple clamps are next.

I unsteadily get upright and on my knees, the movement feeling strange because of the plug in my ass. The coldness hasn't faded and I wonder how that's possible.

Before the clamps, though, Ryder runs his cold fingertips over my nipples. I jerk away, trying to avoid the cold, but he only grins wickedly. I catch sight of Jaxon behind him, looking on with great interests. I pout at them both. Of course I had to fall in love with a couple of dominant sadists. Just my luck.

But I wouldn't change either of them, no way.

Ryder gets each of my nipples nice and hard, then he pulls the clamps, dripping, from the ice water.

I start to say, "Nnnnn—"

He arches an eyebrow. "Are you going to say something? Because I can make this so much worse, Babydoll."

Biting my lip, I shake my head. From behind Ryder, Jaxon laughs softly. Damn them both. I'm going to fill their pillowcases with ice cubes. I'm going to fill their sock drawers with dead fish. I'm going to—

Sharp pain centers on my nipple as Ryder fastens the first clamp.

"Owwww," I whimper.

But as soon as I register the pain, pleasure is fast on its heels and my whimper transforms to a moan.

"Good girl," Ryder murmurs before flicking my second nipple, making sure it's hard.

It is. One hundred percent. Despite the ache and soreness in the first one, and the biting cold, I'm so aroused, my thighs are wet. I watch as Ryder fastens the second clamp and I suck in a breath to keep from saying anything once it's fastened to me.

"So pretty," Ryder says, giving the chain that connects the clamps a little tug.

I moan at the sudden, uncomfortable pull.

"Up again, Babydoll," he says, tugging on the chain for added effect.

I'm quick to scramble to my feet. He leads me by the chain and I try to keep up with his strides to avoid any more uncomfortable tugs on the clamps. Confusion is beginning to stir in me, though; I don't understand why he's doing this. What is this punishment all about?

Probably sensing my growing discomfort, Ryder stops abruptly. He bends and presses his mouth to mine, touching his tongue against my lips until I part them. Then he's kissing the breath out of me, turning me on more than I could've dreamed was possible while wearing a freezing cold plug in my ass and chilly nipple clamps. I want to rub my body against his and increase the tug on my nipples. The pain doesn't matter in the slightest, and in fact, I'd welcome it; I just want to be close to him.

Before I can do anything like that, though, he pulls back and gives me one very brief kiss on the lips.

He whispers against my ear, "Come to the table, little one."

He sets me down in a chair, which is uncomfortable with the plug. A pen and paper rests on the table in front of me. He must have placed them here earlier, while I was begging for Jaxon's cock.

"Did you ever have to write lines in school?" Ryder asks. "You can speak to answer me."

"I'm not sure what you mean," I say.

"You know, like, *I will respect my teacher*, written twenty times, or a hundred times?"

"No, Sir," I say.

"Well, you're going to write some now."

I give him a skeptical look. This sounds like the least sexy punishment I can imagine. Then again, I'd thought the time he made me lean over the table for what felt like forever was a boring punishment, and that had ended up being hot as hell.

"Go ahead," he says.

I raise my hand, like I'm a freaking student in class, because he didn't tell me I could speak to ask questions.

Wearing a handsome-yet-sinful smirk, he says, "Yes, little girl?"

My pussy gives an involuntary squeeze. For some reason, this is really doing it for me. "What should I write, Sir?"

"You'll figure it out," he says. "Oh, wait. I forgot."

Ryder steps into the kitchen area and rifles around in one of the drawers.

I give Jaxon a bewildered look, but he merely comes over to the table and pulls out a chair at the other end before sitting down to watch.

Ryder returns with a piece of string. He ties one end to the pen in front of me, and the other to the chain that connects my nipple clamps.

The length of string between the chain and the pen is not long.

"Go ahead and write something," he says with a cruel smile. "Something you think I would like."

This is impossible—not the act of writing itself, which will merely be difficult and awkward and possibly painful with the chain and clamps—but figuring out what he wants me to write.

Squinting at him, I think for a moment. Then I lean forward and put the pen toward the paper.

Ow, ow, ow. Nope, I won't be able to sit and write.

I raise my hand again.

"Yes, baby girl?" Ryder asks.

"May I stand up and lean over to reach the paper?"

His smile widens. "Yes, you may."

It's still awkward as hell, but I bend over the edge of the table. I'm able to scrawl out, *I will obey Mr. Ryder and Daddy*. There's only minimal tugging on the clamps, and if I'm honest with myself, it feels good.

When I've finished writing the sentence, I send a questioning look to Ryder.

He shakes his head, so I try again. *I will listen to Mr. Ryder and Daddy*.

He shakes his head again.

Shit.

Unable to come up with a new variation, I settle on the truth. *Mr. Ryder and Daddy have amazing cocks and I wish they would fuck me right now*.

Jaxon laughs, but Ryder comes up behind me. I brace

myself for a spanking, and I get one...but not where I expect. His hand comes down hard against my pussy, and a stinging heat radiates between my legs.

I yelp and straighten, but my hand holding the pen doesn't come with my torso, and the tug on my nipples is a whole other kind of pain.

"What? Why, Sir?" I cry.

He spanks my pussy again, this time harder than the first time.

"Ow!" I squeal. "Mr. Ryder! What was that for?"

Ryder glares and spanks my pussy again. "I want you" —he spanks me a third time—"to call me"—another spank—"*Daddy.*"

So that's it. *Mr. Ryder* isn't enough. Our relationship is stronger than it was when we began, and in his mean, sadistic way, he's been trying to tell me that.

My heart aches as I remember all the times I've called him *Sir* or *Mr. Ryder* and his expression darkened, but I never picked up on the why of it.

Well, now I know.

Trying to muster as much dignity as possible when my ass is plugged, my pussy is stinging, and my nipples are throbbing, I turn my head as far as I can.

Looking into Ryder's gorgeous yet stern blue eyes, I say one word. "Daddy."

His mouth is on mine, hot and hungry. He pulls away briefly to murmur, "Good girl," before plundering my mouth again.

12

Ryder

Fuck. She's exquisite.

And now she is really, truly my Babydoll. I dip my tongue in and out of her mouth, imagining that it's my cock, feeling her wet warmth surrounding me. Tugging her to my chest, I revel in the intake of her breath as the nipple clamps press against me. The bite of pain only seems to make her want me more.

This girl was made for me—made for us.

I grab the chain between her nipple clamps and lead her to the bedroom. Jaxon follows, shaking his head. Not in disapproval, but with an expression on his face that says, *It's about fuckin' time.*

Yeah, I know. I was waiting for her to figure it out. I was hoping she'd call me "daddy" without me needing to ask. But I got too impatient, and it doesn't matter, in the end, how she figured it out, because now she knows. And when we make her come with our cocks, I want to hear her scream for her daddies—both of her daddies.

"Hands and knees, up on the bed," I say, letting go of her chain.

She clambers up, her body shaking slightly in anticipation. The plug in her ass has a jeweled base, an iridescent combination of pink and turquoise that made me think of her when I saw it, so I impulsively bought it for her. Tonight, she'll suck Jaxon while I fuck her, because I want to be able to see her ass like this when I come.

"Good job," I say, patting her hip when she's in place. I jerk my head toward Jax, signaling he can join in whenever he wants.

Nodding, he strips off his shirt and climbs on the bed. "You have an idea how you want this to go?" he asks.

"Yeah," I say. "I'm taking her pussy tonight. At least, the first time tonight."

He grins and moves up to Olivia's head. I watch with interest as he touches her lips with his thumb. "Open, Babydoll," he says.

Her mouth opens and he pushes his finger inside.

"Damn, you feel good, little girl," he says. "Nice and warm. Show me what you're going to do to my cock when I fuck your mouth, sweet thing."

While she sucks on his finger, he unfastens his pants and frees his dick. I strip off my shirt and shove off my pants and boxer briefs, then get on the bed behind Olivia. Sometimes, I can't believe this perfect girl is ours. It's like she was made with our kinks in mind. Her lush, spankable ass is right in front of me, and I can't resist bending forward and giving it a gentle nip. Her muffled sound of surprise makes me smile.

I trace my fingers over her skin, reveling in the softness of her. By now, Jax has fed his dick into her mouth, and she's sucking at him enthusiastically. I trail my fingers between her ass cheeks until I reach the jeweled end of the plug. I shake it a little with my hand and Olivia moans. I continue down past the plug until I reach her pussy.

"Fuck, you're so wet," I murmur. "Did you like getting your pussy spanked, Babydoll?"

"You can stop sucking me to answer," Jaxon tells her.

A second later, she says, "Yes, Daddy."

A warm glow of pride and contentment fills my chest. "Yes, Daddy, what?"

"Yes, Daddy," she says, breathless, "I liked it when you spanked my pussy."

"Excellent." Before she can take Jax in her mouth again, I spank her pussy. Her squeal of surprise is music to my ears. "I'm going to spank you a few more times," I say. "Get this naughty pussy all warmed up. But if you so much as drag a tooth over Jaxon's cock, he'll tell me and we'll spank you for real. Understand?"

"Yes, Daddy."

Fuck, hearing her call me *Daddy* is never going to get old.

I spank her a few times, each one landing wet. She moans around Jaxon's cock, but she must be taking extra care because he doesn't complain.

I can't wait any longer. My own dick is feeling sadly neglected. I scoot forward on my knees until I can wipe the head of my cock through Olivia's glistening pussy lips. There's absolutely no reason to wait any longer. Surging inside, I go all the way in, her walls hugging me like a wet, warm glove. It's fucking incredible. I pull out a little before slamming back in.

Olivia moans sweetly. I manipulate the plug and I can feel it moving in her, too. Without warning, Olivia's body tightens and she cries out around Jaxon's cock. I reach around her and rub her clit, and her cries get louder as her orgasm continues.

Jaxon groans and his eyes close as he becomes tense and comes in Olivia's mouth. I'm not ready yet, though, so I stroke through her orgasm, slowly easing in and out during her aftershocks.

Jax sits back to watch, leaning against the head of the bed. "Eyes on me, Babydoll," he says.

I start fucking her harder. "Who are we to you?"

"You're my daddies," she says.

"That's right." I grab her hips and thrust faster. She doesn't complain that I'm hurting her, but I need to be sure. "You're doing okay, Babydoll?"

"Yes, Daddy. I feel great."

I groan and pump faster. "I want you to come again, and I want you to scream for your daddies."

Reaching around her again, I find her slippery little clit.

"Daddy," she moans.

"Yes, that's right, baby girl. Come for us. Come for your daddies." I pinch her clit.

Her pussy pulses around me rhythmically as she comes again, so tight, so swollen.

"Daddy!" she yells. "Daddies! Yes!"

We're hers, and she's ours. I let loose my own release,

filling her up with my come, and with my love, marking this night in my mind forever.

Olivia

"And then what?" Samantha asks, smacking my shoulder. "Don't leave me hanging!"

I've been narrating the events of the past few days—everything about JTS and Daniel—as Samantha and I make our way to the warehouse. I stick out my tongue at her. "Don't you have any appreciation for dramatic tension?"

"No," she says. "Terrence, maybe you'll tell me?"

As soon as she got in the car, she started trying to chat with Terrence, who is sitting in the front passenger seat. It's still not working.

"I'm not here to chat," he says.

"But we're friends," Samantha says, winking at him when he turns around. He's not driving, thankfully—that's Cora's job today.

He's being polite but basically ignoring Samantha's attempts at flirtatious banter. Now, he gives her a dark look and growls, "I'm working."

Samantha's eyes go wide and she turns to me, elbowing me and whispering, "He's so fucking hot."

"He's not a bartender," I say.

She doesn't seem to care, but once I start whispering to her about the other night with Ryder and Jaxon, and all the *daddy* stuff (which she is thankfully very openminded about), she gives me her full attention. Poor Terrence is, for the moment, free of Samantha's grasp.

"And then he spanked me and said he wants me to call him *Daddy*, too," I whisper.

"And then?" she prompts, smacking my shoulder again.

"My bodyguards are going to grab you if you keep hurting me," I say, rubbing my arm.

"Good," she says, "especially if Terrence is the one doing the grabbing."

"You're impossible," I say with a laugh. "Anyway, they also brought up the M-word."

"No way. *Marriage*?" she squeaks.

I nod.

Her eyes are wide with happiness and she drags me into a hug. "You are living the freaking dream, girl!"

We arrive at the warehouse. Terrence jumps out to unlock the gate. Samantha leans forward and says to Cora, "Do I have a chance with him?"

I roll my eyes, but Cora looks thoughtfully between Terrence and Samantha and says, "It's not professional of me to comment on this at all, but...in a different setting, yes. But he'll never do anything while he's working. The man is a machine, I swear."

Samantha's smile lights up the whole interior of the car. "Thanks. I won't bring anything up again during your —or his—working hours."

"Good plan." Cora navigates the car through the open gate, and then parks.

Terrence jogs up to join us. He looks like he's bracing himself for more of Samantha's flirtation, but she doesn't try anything.

I unlock the warehouse door and punch in the numbers for the alarm system. Terrence goes inside while Cora waits with Samantha and me.

A person from beyond the gate rushes in and Cora gets very tense. She mutters, "Someone's approaching," and I realize she must be talking to Terrence through an earpiece.

"It's okay," I hurry to say as soon as I recognize Nate. "It's one of my new employees."

"This wasn't on the schedule," Cora says, not taking her pale green eyes off of Nate.

I shrug. "Well, he's here now and he's passed all of the security checks at Ironwood. I can at least talk to the guy, right?"

"Of course," Cora says.

Nate comes up, waving. "Hi, Olivia!"

"Hey, Nate. This is my friend Samantha Joy, and one of my security team, Cora Fenton."

"Nice to meet you," he says, sticking out his hand. "Nate Boyd."

Samantha shakes with him, but Cora does not. She and Terrence take up stations in the warehouse. Samantha and I face Nate.

"So, what can I do for you?" I ask.

"Oh, well, I was walking past and I saw your car pull in."

"You live around here?" Samantha asks, somewhat rudely.

He shrugs. "Yeah, it's affordable."

"I guess," Samantha says.

I shoot her a look because she sounds super judgmental.

She just shrugs and mouths, *"What?"*

"Anyway," Nate continues, "I just wanted to say hi. What are you up to today?"

I gesture around the warehouse. "There are a few piles of junk left here from the previous owners, and Samantha's going to help me figure out a basic floor plan for when we open up to students and offer classes."

The areas for smaller classes will need to be far away from each other, but we won't have separate rooms because I want everyone to feel safe. I've done a lot of research over the past few days about how to run organizations that involve children or dependants, and one common theme is that no single adult should ever be left alone with kids in a separate area. Even if we completely trust them, even if they've gone through extensive background checks. A lot of times it's a cover-your-ass sort of thing, but I also want to emphasize safety for everyone involved. So, the floor plan has to be open.

"Can I help?" Nate asks. "I don't have anywhere to be right now."

"Oh," I say, surprised. I had figured he would want to go do his own thing. "You're not scheduled to start for another week, but, sure."

Grinning, he sets his messenger bag on the table where I'd conducted the interviews. He claps his hands together. "All right, what are you thinking?"

Samantha gives him a sour look, like he's taking over her role in this endeavor. And to be fair to her, he kind of is. So I'm careful to address *both* of them as I outline my general vision, along with restrictions and other guidelines we need to consider. Cora and Terrence stand off to the side, allowing us space to move around. I put masking tape on the concrete floor to mark various areas, which we'll cordon off with low walls, like the kind that can be bought for offices. But the aim is to always have a line of sight to each area.

At first Samantha is grouchy with Nate, but after a few minutes, he starts trying to flirt with her. I want to tell him not to waste his breath because Samantha has a type and he definitely isn't it. But then, there's a switch in her. I keep watching to see what's up, because no way would she be laughing at his corny lines or allowing him to gently place his hand on her shoulder.

When she smiles at him, I can tell it's definitely fake.

I can't wait until he leaves, so I can talk to her about this.

Bonus, though: Terrence looks like he wants to strangle Nate, and Samantha is completely oblivious; she's too focused on keeping Nate talking and joking around with her.

I keep my smirk to myself—I can't wait to tell Samantha that Terrence was looking jealously on while Nate flirted with her.

After a couple of hours where we struggle to use our imaginations for setting up the room, it's time to go. I'll need to come back with some of those cubicle walls and a few drafting tables, so we can really tell what will be visible yet still give a semblance of quiet areas to promote focused creativity.

Nate gives me a friendly wave. I still have a strange feeling about the guy, so my smile is a little forced as I wave back. He actually presses a kiss to the back of Samantha's hand. I can see her flinch, but I doubt Nate notices it.

He grabs his messenger bag and takes off, and once he's out of earshot, with his back to us, Samantha gives a visible shudder.

"You have to fire him," she says before I can speak.

"What are you talking about?" I ask. "You were encouraging his flirting, Sam, but I could tell you weren't into it at the same time. Tell me what's going on."

Taking my arm, she drags me closer to her. "I was trying to figure out what his deal is."

"He doesn't have a deal! He's been security-checked. Everything's cool."

She shakes her head. "I have a bad feeling."

I open my mouth to retort, but then I close it, because he gives me a bad feeling, too. I've been trying to ignore it, but it's still there.

Samantha's gaze is understanding. "You feel it too, don't you? Your instincts are telling you he's bad news."

"But there's nothing *wrong* with him," I say. "Other than being a little flirty, which doesn't bother me in general—and you were encouraging it. I had to shut him down when we first met. Prior to the interview!" I rush to add. "He did not flirt at the interview, at all. We ran into each other at a coffee shop, first. And when I told him I had a boyfriend, he backed off without acting weird."

"Well, I'm just saying, my gut doesn't like him, so I don't like him." She wipes the back of her hand on her pants as if trying to erase the kiss he'd given her hand in farewell.

All four of us—Samantha, Terrence, Cora, and I—are quiet as we pile into the car and Cora drives us away from the warehouse.

We pass Nate, who's walking down the sidewalk, his messenger bag smacking his thigh with every step.

"That guy," Cora says, tapping the steering wheel thoughtfully. "That guy, I don't like."

I exchange a glance with Samantha.

I'm not sure how to make it happen, because I hate the idea of firing someone, and I don't love conflict. But Nate's got to go.

∼

DADDIES EVER AFTER

1

Olivia

A couple of days go by. I've placed orders for cubicle walls, tables, and chairs for Youth Arts, as well as some comfortable furniture for lounging when students want to hang out or have impromptu, casual meetings. I want the organization's warehouse to feel like an art collective in some ways—a studio where people do their artistic work and also talk shop and collaborate.

Amidst all the preparations for Youth Arts, there's another chore that needs doing.

I need to move out of my studio apartment.

Jaxon and Ryder say it isn't necessary, but to me it is. This studio is a symbol of my fear of abandonment. They might not need to see that symbol demolished, but I do.

Because I'm strong. I'm so strong, and so confident in their love for me, that this doesn't feel like a risk anymore.

And as I look around the tiny apartment, I realize that even at the thought of letting it go, I'm happy. So freaking happy.

I feel as if I could float, because my fear is no longer holding me down.

I barely slept in this bed, which is funny, in a way. I remember the last evening I spent here, when Ryder called me and ordered me to come to the penthouse. That night was the beginning of the three of us truly being together.

And the sex had been so fucking hot.

I give myself a little shake, trying to clear my head so I can focus on the job at hand. Jasmine's still in Pennsylvania, and she's going to hire movers to put her belongings in storage. Most of the things here, especially the big items, like furniture, belong to her.

There's really not much left of mine, at all. I find an earring of mine hiding behind one of Jasmine's picture frames on the dresser, and after I strip the bedding to take it downstairs to the washing machine, I find a prodigal sock at the corner of the bed.

On my way back up the little set of stairs, I wave down at Roman and Squid, my security today. "I have to wait for the laundry to cycle through, okay?"

"No problem, Ms. Santiago," Roman says, and Squid nods in acknowledgment.

I return to the studio and make myself comfortable on the tiny loveseat. Ryder and Jaxon are both at work. Samantha's working today, too. I start to pull up one of my favorite reading apps, but then I remember Jasmine. Now would be the perfect time to chat with her about personal things, if she's available.

Without hesitation, I dial her number.

She answers almost immediately. "Hey! Everything going all right with moving out?"

"Yeah, it's so easy," I say. "I already moved all my stuff to Jaxon's place."

"Lucky little sub," she says, chuckling a little. "You found yourself some nice Doms, didn't you?"

"I'm so lucky," I say. "They keep telling me this is for the long haul, that they're in it forever. I keep waiting for the other shoe to drop...except now, I don't think it will. Everything's perfect, Jasmine, and I'm happy, just a little unsure of myself."

"Unsure how?"

"Do you have a few minutes to talk? I don't want to bug you."

"I have all the time in the world. My Dom is out and instructed me to stay put, so I'm staying put."

"You found someone?" I ask.

"Yep. Don't get too excited. I'm not sure if he's ever going to collar me. But right now, he's exactly what I need."

"I'm so glad," I say. "Where'd you meet?"

"There's a BDSM club, the next city over. There's one in this dinky little town, too, but it kinda sucks. The other one is stricter. More expensive, too, but worth every penny if they make their Doms go through such rigorous training. And they make the subs take classes, too."

"You took classes in being a submissive?" I ask.

"Yep."

"I need those kinds of classes," I say.

"You really don't," Jasmine says. "From what you've told me before about your guys, they know what they're doing, and they've taught you. The beauty in being submissive is the trust you can put in your Dom —or Doms, you lucky slut—and allowing them to push your limits just to the point where it feels amazing, but no further. The classes I had to take were more about that trust, which you already have, and making sure you're not so submissive you never speak up for yourself, a little. But mostly, spotting warning signs during a scene, how to ask for help from someone else, how to avoid bad situations to begin with. Essential skills for someone just starting out. I didn't need them here, but I don't mind the refresher course, especially when I know the club owners are just trying to keep us safe."

I soak in everything that she's saying. It's such a fascinating world. I was peripherally aware of it, because who hasn't heard of *Fifty Shades of Grey*? But I'd never viewed it as something that would be a real part of my life, despite asking Daniel once if he would take more control in the bedroom.

He'd laughed at me, and I'd been afraid to voice my desires since.

I can tell Jaxon and Ryder what I want, though. Because like Jasmine just said, I trust them.

I *am* a lucky slut, I think, grinning.

"Hey, I should go," Jasmine says. "He's back and he's holding up a blindfold and I am so down."

A low voice sounds on her end of the call, and my face heats at the stark command in the tone. Yep, he sounds like a controlling, dominant guy, just like Jaxon and Ryder. Jasmine's going to have fun.

"Yep, talk later," I say. "Have a good time!"

"I will," she says with a laugh. "Call me any time you have questions, okay?"

"Will do. Thanks, Jasmine."

I didn't learn anything new from our conversation, but I feel completely justified in moving out of this apartment and allowing the landlord to rent it out to someone else. It served me well, as my emergency fall-back option.

But I really don't need it anymore.

Once the bedding is finished in the washer and dryer, I fold it and stack it neatly on the bed for the movers. Then I lock up and leave, whispering a quiet thank-you to this apartment that I no longer need.

Jaxon

When I get home from work, Olivia is pacing around the kitchen island, looking perplexed.

"Everything okay?" I ask.

She shrugs. "Yes? No? I have to fire a guy that I just hired. He hasn't even technically started working yet."

"What has he done wrong?"

"That's the thing. He hasn't done anything wrong. Do I need grounds to fire him?"

I shake my head. "Not in California, you don't. As long as you aren't discriminating against him or breaking a contract you have with him."

"I'm not doing either of those things," she says before resuming her pacing.

"Can I ask why you're firing this man?"

"It's not logical," she says, chewing her lip.

"That's okay."

"Not really. I had a whole system set up to be fair to everyone, and he was in the top three candidates based on my rubric. But I just have this bad feeling."

"So he failed the gut check," I say.

"Not just mine, but Sam's, too," she says. "And Cora's."

"Cora didn't like him?"

"Nope. Neither did Terrence. But that might be because Nate was flirting with Sam, and I think Terrence might be interested in Sam—"

"Wait, what?" I ask.

She grins impishly at me. "Yep. Budding romance between my bestie and my bodyguard."

"Are you serious? Because that's grounds for me to fire Terrence."

"Oh! No. I'm not serious. Well, crap." She holds her finger up in a *wait a minute* gesture, then takes a deep breath. "Sam has a thing for Terrence and she's been trying to flirt with him, but he shuts it down every single time. He's been nothing but professional. But he looked pissed off when Nate and Samantha were flirting the other day, so I'm hoping he might secretly like her. But it could also be that he just doesn't like Nate—maybe Nate failed Terrence's gut check, too."

"Nate got through the screening process?" I ask.

She nods.

Maybe I'll have Lin do a little extra investigation on the guy. I don't like that he's raising everyone's hackles.

Olivia still looks bothered.

"For what it's worth," I say, "I think you're making the right call in firing this man."

"You do? Even though it isn't a logical decision?"

"My gut instincts have saved me more than once," I say. "I think you should listen to yours. Is there anything I can do to help?"

"Can you just...sit with me and hold my hand?" she asks, looking over her shoulder at me as she walks to the living room.

"Of course. You know, people get fired all the time. Employees don't work out for whatever reason." I sit down with her on the couch and take her hand.

She takes a deep breath. "Okay, I'm going to call him. No, actually, I'm going to text him. I should fire him in person, at least. So I'm just texting for a meeting."

She's so cute, especially when she's flustered. But within that, she's genuinely stressed, and I hate that. "I have to offer," I say. "Do you want me to text him for you? Or fire him for you? Babydoll, I'll do whatever you want —you know that, right?"

Her smile is sweet, genuine. "I know that, Daddy. Thank you. But I need to do this, and get practice in it. It's probably not the first time I'll have to fire someone."

She shudders at the idea, and I grab her into a quick hug.

"Best to just get it done, then," I say. "Ask to meet him tomorrow and give him a time. That way he can agree if it works, and you don't have to do a lot of back and forth over it."

"Good idea," she says, then types out a message on her phone. The device gives a little *bloop* sound as a text comes in immediately. "That's him," she says. "He agreed to ten a.m. Oh wait, he's typing something else."

She holds out her phone screen, so I wait with her,

watching the little ellipsis that shows a new message is coming. Finally, the message pops up.

Actually, I forgot I have a thing going all day. I could meet after eight, or the following day.

Olivia scrunches her nose at me. "I don't want to put this off any longer than necessary."

She types, *Eight works for me. See you at the warehouse.*

See you then, he responds.

"Okay." Olivia heaves a huge sigh. "Will you fuck me now, so I don't have to think about any of that until tomorrow?"

Laughing, I gently take her phone from her hands and set it on the coffee table.

Her gasps and moans as I eat her out are a song I will never grow tired of.

Olivia

My bodyguards tonight are Terrence and Cal. Terrence is behind the wheel, and Cal sits next to him. While Terrence is aloof as always, Cal cracks jokes as we go down Caro Boulevard toward the warehouse. "And on your right, you'll find yet another boutique catering to the crusty uppercrust of San Esteban...a boutique full of dog toys that may cost more than your dog."

In the back seat, I snicker.

Encouraged, Cal goes on, "Nobody asked for this boutique, and yet here it stands, a proud testament to dogs ruling the earth. Which is as it should be."

Soon, though, we travel far enough down Caro Boulevard that the boutiques pass out of sight and we're now surrounded by industrial buildings and rundown apartment complexes. Cal's narration halts as he stares out at a collection of battered tents beneath an underpass. "I can't make fun of that," he murmurs.

When we reach the warehouse, Cal gets out of the car and unlocks the gate.

I haven't been to the warehouse at night before, and it's a little spooky. Thankfully, one of the first measures I took in cleaning up the exterior was putting up several lights. Jaxon and Ryder had cameras installed, also, and they're hooked up to the system at Ironwood. Most are hidden, so even if someone comes in and disables the visible ones, Ironwood employees will be able to monitor the secret camera feeds.

Nate isn't here yet, which is disappointing. I want to get this done and over with as soon as possible. I've spent the entire day nervously walking around Jaxon's penthouse. He and Ryder did an excellent job of keeping me distracted last night, but they both had work today.

A text flashes on my phone, beneath Ryder's name. *You can do this, Babydoll.*

Jaxon texts immediately after. *We're saving up all kinds of good things to reward you when you're done.*

My heart feels gooey and warm at the thought of these tender men and their encouragement. I love them so freaking much. I didn't know it was possible to love anyone this much.

Terrence and I get out of the car and go inside, where I disarm the system and then we wait.

Cal intercepts someone walking toward the warehouse—I can see them through the door, which Terrence and I left open for Cal. The two share a conversation that I can't hear, and then the guy walks off. Cal makes his way into the warehouse.

"What was that about?" I ask.

"It's a guy who lives around here," Cal says. "He's wondering about all the activity here and was asking what the warehouse will be used for."

"Oh, cool," I say.

My stomach is doing repeated somersaults. It's five minutes to eight and I wish Nate would get here already.

Fifteen minutes go by. I walk in circles around the table, then force myself to sit down and take deep breaths. Another fifteen minutes go by. I check my phone repeatedly.

At eight thirty, I send Nate a text. *Are you coming to our meeting?*

No response.

I look over at Terrence and Cal, who are standing quietly near the door. "I guess he's a no-show," I say. "Let's head out."

All of that nervous anxiety for nothing. I've been worked up all day, and yes, I know that Nate isn't responsible for my feelings—*I* am. But at the same time, if he'd come here, I'd be all done with those feelings and moving on to hiring the next person on my list, or possibly creating another call for applicants.

We're in the car, driving down the sketchier part of Caro Boulevard, when Terrence swears.

"Get in the middle seat, Olivia," he barks.

He used my first name. Weird. I quickly unbuckle and do as he said.

"Buckle in again. Now." He doesn't turn around to

glance at me, but his eyes flicker toward the rearview mirror repeatedly. He's looking at someone behind us.

"We're being followed?" I ask, my voice going high with fear. I clear my throat and say, more normally, "Is there anything I can do?"

Cal turns around in his seat. His kind, brown eyes are serious. "Keep your head down. Stay quiet if you can, so Terrence can concentrate."

I nod, scooting down in my seat, and he looks past me.

"They're coming up on our right," he says to Terrence in a tight voice.

"I know."

"Speed up," Cal says.

"I'm fucking trying."

The engine roars. My heart thunders in my chest. I'm helpless back here, unable to do a damn thing.

I can call Jaxon and Ryder, though.

The car swerves, and my phone flies out of my hand. I hold back my scream.

"This is going to get rough," Terrence says, and I'm not sure if he's talking to me or Cal. "They're going to hit us."

"Hang on, Olivia," Cal says. "I'm coming back there."

"Wait, what?" I ask. "No, stay up there."

"This is my job," he says, climbing between the front seat, his movements awkward. The car swerves again and he has to brace against his seat so he doesn't fly into my lap.

A quick glimpse out the right window shows me dark figures in a dark car. I can't identify it from here, and I want to do as I was told, keep my head down. What if they have guns? Who the hell is doing this?

Cal makes it to the rear bench seat, placing himself on my right, between me and the other car. He grabs for his safety belt just as something smashes into the door.

The squeal of tires and crunch of metal assaults my eardrums, louder than anything I've ever heard, and then everything is dead silent.

2

Ryder

Marinara sauce and meatballs are simmering on the stove, and a bottle of wine is open and airing out on the counter with three glasses. The noodles are rinsed and ready to cook. Olivia told me her comfort food is spaghetti and meatballs, so as soon as she gets home from her meeting with that Nate guy, she'll be treated. I'm hoping this will be a good way for her to unwind.

I want to be a good boyfriend to her, not just a Dom who can satisfy her sexual cravings.

My phone buzzes on the kitchen island. Expecting a text from Olivia, I'm surprised to see Terrence's personal code, with a dash followed by two nines. There's trouble.

My stomach falls. I turn off the stove and text back, *Location?*

It takes him an eternity to respond, but finally words appear on the screen. *Caro 8*

I have to assume he means Caro Boulevard and Eighth Street.

I pause only to put on shoes, and I dial Jax as I get into the elevator and jab the button for the parking garage. Jaxon's probably at Ironwood, or on his way home.

He answers immediately. "What is it?"

"Trouble. Terrence texted. I don't know what's going on, but the location is Caro and Eighth. Where are you?"

"Just pulled into the parking garage."

"Wait for me there, the elevator just arrived." As the doors slide open, I see his car idling close by, so I jog over to it and slide into the passenger seat.

"Talk to me," he says.

"I don't have anything except the address. Calling Ironwood now." Protocol dictates all emergency messages go straight to the office, but in any matter concerning Olivia, Terrence was right to tell me or Jaxon first.

Olivia better be okay. She has to be. And as soon as I get her, it's going to be hard not to lock her in the penthouse until the end of time, because the girl has a knack for getting in trouble.

No, that's not fair. Shit keeps happening. She's not inviting it—she has enemies. Too many of them.

Squid's at the office tonight, a spare guard, and he answers the phone. I recite my security code to verify I'm really me, and then I say, "What's happening?"

"We don't know yet," he says. "The car crashed. Terrence's earpiece isn't working, and Cal's isn't, either. Or they aren't responding. The last they checked in, they were leaving the warehouse. I'm heading over there with Roman right now. We've already called nine-one-one."

"They're on Caro and Eighth," I say. "Terrence messaged me."

"Gotcha. We'll go there instead. I'll get emergency services up to date, too."

There's nothing else to say. We end the call and I glance over at Jaxon. His jaw is tight, and his hands are white-knuckled on the steering wheel.

I want to yell at him to drive faster, but he's already going as fast as he can.

Olivia, baby, we're coming.

Olivia

Cal isn't moving. His body is crumpled on the other side of the car. My chest hurts like hell, and it takes a minute for me to realize it's because the seatbelt is cutting across my torso. The car landed on its side. If I unbuckle, I need to be careful that I don't fall directly onto Cal. But I can't remain like this.

Bracing myself on the front seats, I unsnap the buckle.

Relief.

My neck is killing me, but I shove aside the pain. Probably whiplash from the impact.

"Cal," I whisper.

There's nothing happening beyond the car, but I can't see much. Are those people still here, the ones who hit us?

"Terrence?" I say.

A groan comes from the front seat.

"Terrence, Cal's not moving," I say.

No response. Terrence must be hurt, too.

Placing my feet and arms carefully, I maneuver down to Cal. I put my hand on his chest and wait. An unsteady breath, then another.

Thank God, he's alive. I can't see what's wrong with him—he doesn't seem to be bleeding. What can I do for him? Nothing. Shit. I've never felt so useless, so helpless.

"Terrence, do you need anything?" I ask.

"Stay...down," he says, his voice raspy.

"Okay," I whisper.

The car moves, like someone is climbing up onto it. I look up, out the side window which is now facing the sky.

A face appears. I hold back a scream. He uses something—the butt of a gun?—to smash open the window, and the glass rains down onto Cal and me.

Lights illuminate him, a strobe effect like an ambulance or police car. The man disappears.

I clutch Cal's hand, which feels far too cold.

The next face to appear in the window is brightly lit and they're holding a flashlight. It briefly blinds me and I cover my face.

"Sorry about that," a woman's voice says. "I'm Officer Erica Voight. We're going to get you out of there. Who else is in the car with you?"

"My bodyguards," I say. "Terrence Johnson and Cal Romanoff. They're both unconscious, they need help. Please."

"The EMTs are here," the officer says. "Hang tight."

I should feel comforted by the officer's caring and professional tone, but I don't feel truly safe until I'm out of the car and Jaxon and Ryder are on either side of me, their body heat warming me while I give a statement to the officer.

Cal and Terrence are both bundled into ambulances. The EMTs checked me out, and I don't even have a concussion. It doesn't seem fair that Cal and Terrence were hurt, and I barely have a scratch. I'm relieved, and then I feel guilty for that relief, and all I want to do is climb into bed and cry for the next week.

Jaxon

This was too fucking close. Again. I can't stand this, Olivia being in trouble all the time. My heart's breaking, over and over again, a fucking crack in my chest with acid poured over it.

A part of me wants to lash out at the universe. A part of me wants to lash out at her, yell at her for leaving the house and putting herself in danger yet again. If she just stayed in the penthouse, I could keep her safe.

But it's unreasonable. I know this. So I hold tight to her while Ryder drives my car. He seemed to sense that I was about to lose it—my mind, my temper, I don't know. And he told me to get in the back seat with Olivia.

She's terrified as we drive down Caro back toward Dorado Heights. Shivering. She clings to my arm. I wonder if she's picking up on my rage. I'm trying to rein it in. I'm not mad at her, not really. But I'm scared because we could've lost her.

We might lose Cal. He's in critical condition. Terrence has a concussion but he's stable.

Cal, though.

I'm worried. And it could've just as easily been Olivia being strapped to a gurney and rushed to the hospital. Again.

She's the only thing keeping me grounded right now. If she wasn't holding onto my arm, I'd be burning with rage and smashing things.

"Daddy?" she says, her voice small.

I force my jaw to relax and I look down at her. Those gray eyes of hers are full of tears. "Hey, Babydoll. What is it?"

"You're mad," she says.

"Not at you, sweetheart."

"I'm mad, too," she whispers. "And scared."

"Don't worry, we're going to protect you."

"Not scared for me," she says, some new steel in her voice. "I'm worried about Cal. Does he have family? Should we call them?"

"It's already taken care of," I say. "They were notified as soon as we found out there was an accident. His brother is meeting him at the hospital."

"And what about Terrence?" she asks.

Ryder speaks from the front seat. "We tried to get in touch with his ex-wife, but she's not available. Squid is going to wait at the hospital and give him a ride home if they release him."

"Okay," Olivia says.

She turns away from me, then, and stares blankly out the window. I grab her hand and twine my fingers with hers, although she barely seems to register the touch. My anger cools into concern. I know she has a tendency to shut down when things get too overwhelming, but I don't like what's happening to her now.

"You need to talk to us, Olivia," I say.

She shakes her head. "Not now."

Ryder pulls into the parking garage. Once we're parked, I get out of the car and reach for Olivia. She takes my hand again, but there's no pressure, no life to it.

"Nope, Babydoll, you have to stay with us," I say.

She just nods.

I exchange a look with Ryder, then lift Olivia into my arms. She automatically wraps her legs around my waist.

"We're going to get you into a nice bath," Ryder says, rubbing her shoulder as we step into the elevator.

"And we'll get some dinner in your tummy," I add.

"Does that sound good?" Ryder asks.

"No. Cal and Terrence aren't having dinner or a bath right now."

"Nothing we do right now will help Cal and Terrence," I say as the elevator takes us up. "It fucking sucks, Olivia, but there is absolutely nothing we can do except wait for the doctors and nurses to do their jobs. Refusing to care for yourself accomplishes nothing."

I lean back so I can look into her face. Her chin wobbles and she squeezes her eyes shut.

"Eyes on me, sweetheart," I say.

It takes her a moment, but she opens her eyes. Her face twists and she lets out a sob. "I don't deserve to cry," she says. "I'm not hurt, *they* are."

"Oh, babe. Let yourself cry. Let it out."

She finally does. We reach the penthouse and she buries her face in my shoulder and her body shakes as she lets out all of the emotions she's feeling.

Ryder goes straight to the bathroom and begins running a bath. I carry Olivia there, rubbing circles on her back. Once the tub is filled, I start to help her out of her clothes, but she keeps trying to push my hands away.

"I don't want to get in the bath," she says. "I don't want any of this, it's wrong after everything that—that happened…"

Ryder kicks off his shoes, sets his phone and wallet on the counter, and climbs into the bath, fully clothed. I gape at him in surprise, and Olivia does, too.

He cocks his head and stares hard at her. "*Now* will you get in?"

"What are you doing?" Olivia asks, stunned out of her protests.

"Come on, Babydoll," he says. "Accept this. Accept that we love you and we want to care for you. Accept that we were scared out of our goddamned minds tonight and we need you as much as you need us."

She nods, and when I undress her, she doesn't try to bat away my hands anymore. As soon as she's naked, I hold her hand while she climbs into the tub. Ryder pulls her back against his chest. She plucks at the soaked fabric of his jeans. "These are going to be difficult to remove."

"Maybe I'll sleep in them like this," he drawls.

Olivia just shakes her head, a little smile forming on her face. Then she seems to remember the accident, and her smile disappears.

"Talk to us, sweetheart," I say. "Tell us what you're feeling."

"I don't know how to feel," she says. "I'm just…I'm so sad and scared, but I'm relieved to be alive, but I don't deserve it."

"You *do* deserve to be alive," Ryder says, hugging her close and kissing the side of her head. "I can't handle the thought of something bad happening to you."

My phone buzzes in my pocket, and I rush to fish it out. The text on the screen provides some relief, and I hold it up to show Olivia.

"There," I say, "see? Terrence has already been released from the hospital."

She lets out a shuddering exhale. "And Cal?"

I don't have a good feeling about Cal. I'm going to need to go to the hospital—it's the least I can do. But all I say to Olivia right now is, "No word yet on Cal."

Olivia

It's the next morning after the accident.

No, it wasn't an accident. It was an attack. The men in that other car attacked Terrence, Cal, and me. No "accident" about it.

Jaxon's at the hospital, waiting for Cal to get out of surgery. He had massive internal bleeding and is still in critical condition.

I wish there was something I could do.

All I can think about are the random jokes he would tell. Just yesterday, he was narrating Caro Boulevard like some bizarre tour guide. But he was sensitive, too, to the struggles of the unhoused people in the Bellefleur District.

Ryder and I are sitting close together on the sofa in

the living room. Our phones are close by, because we're both waiting for Jaxon to update us on Cal.

"We should go to the cabin," he says.

"Not right now," I say.

"Obviously not right now. Maybe this weekend, though."

"I'm not going anywhere until we know Cal is going to be okay," I say. "Hopefully I'll be able to visit him after the surgery."

Ryder squeezes my knee, his hand warm through my leggings. "Of course, Babydoll."

My phone gives a little *ping* on the coffee table, and I hurry to grab it. Nate's name flashes on the screen, followed by a text. *So sorry I missed you last night. I came at nine, then looked at my phone and realized it was supposed to be eight. Rain check?*

Before I can respond, Ryder snatches my phone. "There will be no rain check," he growls. "I can write the text, or you can."

I can't resist sticking my tongue out at him. "Is that an order, Daddy?"

"Yes, it fucking is." He holds out my phone. "You or me?"

"I'll do it," I say, and take the phone from him.

I was in an accident and I'm recovering, I write. *There won't be a new meeting. I won't be employing you after all. Please send me your PayCheck email, and I'll provide you with a $300 payment for your time blocking out the warehouse floor plan with me the other day.*

Before I hit *send*, I hold the phone up to Ryder. "Does this meet your standards, Your Highness?"

"Princess, you are on thin fucking ice," he says.

Humming to myself, I send the message to Nate.

As soon as that message disappears, another message comes in, this one from Jaxon. He has sent it to both me and Ryder at the same time.

Cal didn't make it.

All the air is sucked from the room and I reach blindly for Ryder.

3

Ryder

Olivia sits between Jaxon and me while the officiant drones on at the front of the church. The officiant isn't talking about anything real. He isn't talking about Cal. He's just philosophizing on the meaning of life and death.

Two days ago, we lost a good man, a dedicated man. He was guarding Olivia, and he knew the risks of the job, just like we all do. But we never think it's going to happen to us.

The officiant finishes his spiel, and then Cal's brother gets up and says a few words. A couple of Cal's friends speak, and then Jaxon stands up.

"Cal was a good man. He died while protecting someone important to me, and for that, I'll be forever grateful. He was brave, but he was also funny, and caring. I know"—Jax clears his throat and his eyes are red with unshed tears—"I know this probably isn't a comfort to everyone mourning him. But Cal died as he lived—a hero who protected the people around him."

Olivia gives a quiet sob, and I squeeze her hand.

When we leave the church, she stops in front of Cal's brother.

"Eric, is it?" she asks.

He nods.

"Cal...Cal saved my life," she says. "I'll never forget him."

Eric's face crumples and he leans forward, grabbing Olivia in a hug, and he sobs against her shoulder. She cries, too.

Jaxon and I wait, allowing them their cry, hoping that the cathartic moment will help heal both of their hearts. My own chest aches. It's a different kind of pain. I'm grateful Olivia's alive. I'm grateful Cal was there.

But it never should've fucking happened.

After the funeral, I drive us out of the city.

"Where are we going?" Olivia asks.

"The cabin," I say.

"But all my stuff—"

"We packed it for you already, Babydoll," Jaxon says next to her in the back seat.

She nods, then curls up against him, staring out the window at the scenery passing by. Eventually, she falls asleep. I hope her dreams are a respite from the sorrow of reality.

Ryder

I think the cabin helps, although it's hard to tell. Three days pass. None of us feels like working, but Jaxon and I sneak moments in. Between the two of us, we're in almost constant contact with our folks at Ironwood, and Jaxon's detective friend, Baldwin, is in touch as well. He isn't working the case, but he's keeping us in the loop as much as possible.

Olivia wants us all sleeping together each night. I have absolutely no problem with this. Breathing in her sweet scent, touching her soft skin, reassuring myself that she's okay, she's healthy and whole. Maybe not happy, not right now. But we're working on it.

Jaxon

Leonie's voice is firm on the other end of the line. "There's no direct link. No evidence."

"There's got to be *something*," I say. "Put Lin on."

"She'll tell you the same thing," Leonie says.

"Put her on."

Leonie puts me on hold and her sigh is cut off. A few seconds later, Lin answers. "Rosewood here."

"Lin," I say, "is any progress being made at all?"

She clicks her tongue. "We don't have anything firm. I'm looking at headshots of three dozen people from that protest. Maybe if Olivia looked them over...? Terrence doesn't recognize any of them, but Olivia's the real connection."

I don't want to ask that of Olivia, and I can hear her talking in low tones with her therapist from the other room. The grief counselor offers telephone appointments, and this is Olivia's second meeting.

"I'll ask her when she's free," I say. "In the meantime, walk me through it again."

"There was the fire at the mom's house," she says. "JTS was tracking Olivia via the chip in her purse, and they could've easily set that up. Their aim did seem to be murder, although that failed. Due, in part, to the sudden appearance of Daniel Pinoir. So far I've found nothing that would connect him to any of the necessary weapons to tranquilize the guards and the mother and then start the fire. JTS and its supporters is so large, it would be easy for them to obtain the weapons and supplies—even the accelerant—without raising anyone's alarms. Daniel Pinoir is one man working alone, as far as we can tell. I don't think he's behind it."

I don't think he is, either. But it's nice to go over it once more and know that I'm not alone in my thinking.

"How about the accident that killed Cal?" I ask.

"We know Olivia wasn't being tracked," Lin says. "She brought by her phone as you asked, and Leonie checked it out. There's nothing in it. Her purchase of the warehouse would be a matter of public record, however. But the attack came late in the evening; no one would expect to her to be there that late. If they wanted to stake it out, though, again, JTS has the manpower. But Pinoir could just as easily be following her around."

"Do you think he was behind the accident?" I ask, pinching the bridge of my nose.

"Are you asking what I can prove, or what I think?"

I sigh. "I'm asking what you think."

"I don't think it's his style, based on his previous inter-actions with her. Everything had been personal. Wrecking her apartment. Destroying her sculptures. Kidnapping. A car accident doesn't harm anything personal to her, and it doesn't come into physical contact with her. It doesn't fit his pattern."

"So we're back to JTS," I say. "Have you kept tabs on Genevieve Warren?"

"Her social media postings have dropped off in the past two days," she says, "but as of six days ago, when the accident took place, she was in the south of France."

"She could've arranged this from there," I say.

"It's possible." Lin sounds skeptical.

Fuck, I'm skeptical, too. Vehicular assault isn't Genevieve's style, either. She's much more likely to cause public embarrassment or shame, not physically attack someone. And Ryder and I were pretty clear—it's never going to happen with either of us and her again.

"Have you looked into the Nate guy who was supposed to meet Olivia at the warehouse that night?" I ask.

"I have," Lin says, "and the police have, too. He's clean. Maybe a little too clean."

"He's with JTS, I just know it," I say.

"We don't have proof."

Fuck proof, I want to say, but instead I force myself to take a deep breath. Losing my shit isn't going to help this matter. "Keep looking," I say.

"Okay," Lin says. "And I have some unsolicited advice."

"Yeah?"

"Yeah. I think you three should return to the city. The cabin wouldn't be hard for JTS to find. They have plenty of connections and my guess is they're looking for ways to get to the congresswoman through her daughter. You could ask more of the guards to go to where you are, but..."

"But it's harder for them to do their job here, I get it," I say. We have a few guards with us, stationed on the property and staying in a rental when they're off-duty. But it's not a huge crew. "I'll think it over."

I've already made the decision, actually, but I should talk it over with Ryder and Olivia. Olivia seems to recharge here—it worked after Daniel kidnapped her, and getting away from the city is good for all of us from time to time.

But not if it carries such risks.

Lin sends me the isolated stills of people from the protest, so I go into the kitchen where Ryder is cooking, to wait for Olivia to finish her therapy session.

The kitchen smells like spices and peppers and my stomach rumbles in anticipation.

"Anything new from Ironwood?" Ryder asks, opening the oven and peering inside at a glass platter full of enchiladas.

"Nothing new, really," I say. "Lin wants Olivia to look over all of the people we could isolate from the protest footage. I'm suspicious of that Nate guy and I'm having Lin do another check on him. He knew Olivia would be at the warehouse that night. He's the only one who could've known."

"We trust everyone at Ironwood, right?" Ryder says.

"Yes." There's no question in my mind.

"Okay. And Genevieve?"

"She was still in Europe at the time of the accident."

He nods. "She's obviously insane, but I don't think she would do this."

"She wouldn't. She's capable of a lot, but not this."

Ryder rubs his hands over his face. "I need Olivia to be okay. I can't stand it...I'm so goddamn worried, Jax."

"I know. Me, too."

Speak of the cute little devil, and she wanders right in. Her eyes look a little red, as if she's been crying, and I pull her into a hug, kissing the top of her head and inhaling her scent.

"How'd your session go?" Ryder asks.

She shrugs. "It was okay. I feel a little better after talking, and a little worse."

"Do you feel up to looking at some pictures of people, and seeing if you recognize any of them?" I ask.

"If it puts us closer to finding out who's behind this, and responsible for Cal's death?" Her voice turns fierce and hard. "Absolutely."

I pull out my phone and set it up for Olivia. She swipes through the images Lin sent, frowning.

"I don't recognize any of these people." She passes my phone back.

I was hoping she'd see that Nate guy in the crowd, even though I'm positive Lin would've already had the other guards look over the stills, including Terrence, who's met Nate. "All right, then we're done."

"I can look again," she says, reaching for the phone.

I hold it out of her reach. "Nope. All through."

"I want to help," she says.

Ryder speaks up. "You're stressed enough as it is."

"I'm not stressed." She takes a long, deep breath and lets it out slowly. "See?"

I spin her around and run my fingers and thumb over the back of her neck. "You're as tense as ever. Maybe you need a massage."

"Like that one you gave me when the three of us tried watching a movie?" she says, a playful lilt in her voice.

"Yeah, maybe something like that," I say, my dick springing to life. This is the first time she's so much as hinted at fucking.

"Dinner first," Ryder says. "I didn't work my ass off in here just so we can...aw, hell, Babydoll, what are you doing?"

She's lowering to her knees on the floor in front of him and peering up at him with pleading eyes.

He sends me a helpless look. "I hope you weren't too hungry, Jax. Dinner's going to be late."

"I can see a good appetizer right here," I say. "Babydoll, take your clothes off."

Ignoring me, she reaches for Ryder's belt.

So she wants to play.

Making a *tsk* sound of disappointment—which is all pretend, because I'm the opposite of disappointed right now—I stalk over to her and wrap my hand in her silken ponytail. Carefully, so I don't hurt her, I lift until she has no choice but to rise up off her knees and stand with me.

I reward her with a kiss, forcing my tongue into her mouth and sliding it against hers, tasting her for the first time in days. When I pull back from the kiss, Olivia's eyes are half-closed.

"Daddy," she whispers.

"Babydoll," I say, my voice stern.

Her eyes widen.

Grinning, I spin her around so she's facing the kitchen island. Then I yank down her leggings and pop her on the ass.

"Ouch!" she yells. "Why?"

"You know why," I say. "If you disobey, you get a spank."

She looks over her shoulder at Ryder. "Daddy?"

"You want me to save you from Jax?" He gives a sadistic laugh. "Not fucking likely, baby girl. Disobedient brats get punished."

"I thought you would've *wanted* me to suck your cock," she grouses.

"Oh, you'll be sucking it," he says, grabbing himself through his sweatpants.

"But we'll have dinner first, as planned," I say.

Olivia turns her head so she can look at me. "But I want you both now, not later."

"Well, if you're not interested later, that's okay," I say. "But you're not getting our cocks now. You didn't get naked when I told you, and now you must face the consequences."

"Fine." She rolls her eyes and moves to pull up her pants.

I grab her wrist and hold it fast. "Oh, you misunderstood."

Her questioning look is all innocence and surprise.

"You," I say, putting her hand back on the counter and giving her ass another spank, "won't be moving a muscle unless we tell you to, throughout dinner. And that spank just now was for rolling your eyes at me. Don't push me, Babydoll; I'm just getting warmed up."

The sarcasm is heavy in her voice as she says, "Oh, I wouldn't *dream* of pushing you."

"It's almost like she *wants* to be punished," Ryder says with false wonder. "I'll be right back. Get her undressed from the waist down. Or all of her, I don't care."

Now the little brat looks nervous, and I chuckle. I help her out of her pants and panties, giving her another spank when she wiggles her ass. I'm just tugging off her long-sleeved tee when Ryder returns, holding a new toy, still in its packaging. The toy is made of a knobbed panel. It's hot pink and comes with matching, adjustable straps.

"What's that?" Olivia asks.

He holds it up. "A vibrator you can wear with a harness. And we keep the controller."

Olivia's pretty lips curve downward in a frown. She can see this is going to be fun, but whether it's more fun for us or for her...well, it'll be fun for all of us.

"Don't worry," I tell her, smoothing a hand over her brow. "We'll never be too sadistic. Probably."

But I know where this is going. Orgasm denial.

Ryder gets the toy out of its package and washes off the little vibrator panel. He untangles the harness and says, "Lift up your right leg, Babydoll."

Olivia does, and he pulls up one part of the hot pink harness, then he taps her left ankle and she allows him to tug up the other side.

"I don't like this, I don't think this is going to be good for me," she mutters.

Ryder rubs his stubbled cheek against her hip, then presses a kiss there while he tightens the harness in place. "Turn around, little one, let's see how pretty you look."

The panel is pressed securely to her mound. She stands uncertainly before us, wearing only her bra and the harness.

"Fuck, you're beautiful," I whisper.

"And you're about to be very, *very* frustrated," Ryder says.

She shrugs a shoulder, trying to look indifferent as she says, "I'm not worried."

I hold back my laugh.

Ryder pulls the enchiladas out of the oven and says, "Why don't you have a seat at the table, Babydoll?"

She's halfway there before I grab the vibrator's controller and turn it to the lowest level. Olivia freezes mid-step, then continues on, her gait slightly awkward, but determined.

I take two of the plates Ryder serves up to the table, where a green salad is already waiting, dressed in olive oil and smelling faintly of lemon.

"How much salad do you want, sweetheart?" I ask Olivia.

Her lips are pressed tightly together.

"Answer me," I say.

"Um, some," she says, her voice breathy.

I calmly add some to her plate, then to mine. Ryder joins us with his plate and picks up his silverware.

We look perfectly domestic here at the round dining room table. Except for the fact that two of us are completely dressed while the third is almost naked and about to come.

4

Jaxon

I reach for the vibrator's controller and nudge the intensity down to its lowest setting. Olivia gives me a pout. After taking a bite of my enchilada, I turn the vibrator off entirely. She sighs, and I can't tell if she's relieved or disappointed.

"Aren't you hungry, Olivia?" Ryder asks solicitously.

She gives him a weak smile and picks up her fork.

He allows her to take a few bites, then he reaches for the controller and turns on the vibrator again. The low buzz is audible in the quiet room. Olivia is so fucking cute because she's trying to pretend it has no effect on her.

But Ryder just lets the vibrator do its work. He and I both largely ignore Olivia, even though she starts squirming in her seat.

She drops her fork, and I look up.

She's really getting into it now, her chest heaving, her hips rolling back and forth in her chair.

"Touch your tits," I tell her, my voice gruff. "Play with your nipples."

She does as I ask without complaint, and her gasps and moans grow loud in the quiet dining room. Her hands are braced on the edge of the table, her body beginning to tense up.

Ryder turns off the vibrator.

"Fuck!" Olivia shouts. "No! Turn it back on. Please, Daddy."

"In a minute," Ryder says, setting down the controller and taking a bite of his enchilada.

Olivia makes a pitiful little whimpering sound. Her dismay turns me on, but not as much as her eventual climax will—that's going to be a thing of fucking beauty, because it's going to be absolutely incredible for her.

"Eat your dinner," I tell her. "You're going to need your strength."

She gives me an "oh shit" look of trepidation, and Ryder and I both grin.

The next twenty minutes are spent in orgasm-denying fun, pushing Olivia to the edge, then yanking her back again. After the fourth time of nearly getting her there, she stands up.

"Please. I need something in my pussy. I can warm your cocks, I can suck you while the other one fucks me, anything."

"She gets pretty vocal about what she wants when we get her amped up," Ryder says to me.

"Yeah, it's a new side of her," I say. Turning to Olivia, I push out my chair and put my hand on my thigh. "You want something in your pussy? Ride my fingers, Babydoll."

"But I want your cock, Daddy."

"You haven't earned my cock."

She comes around the table and sits on my leg, pressing her pussy over my fingers and against my thigh. Her slick heat on my hand makes my cock throb in my pants. Ryder starts up the vibrator again, and Olivia gasps. She pushes her hips back and forth, taking in my fingers faster, harder. Her body starts to tense up. Her moans increase.

Ryder turns off the vibrator and I pull my fingers out of her.

Olivia wordlessly shakes her head and makes a frustrated scream.

"Sorry?" I say. "What are you trying to tell me?"

A tear rolls down her cheek as she looks between Ryder and me. "Please, Daddies. Please. Please, please let me come. I'll do anything."

"Oh, little one," Ryder tuts. "Let's see what we can do for you."

Olivia

This damned vibrator and harness are going straight into the garbage as soon as my daddies aren't looking.

It feels so good and yet I'm about to cry, or scream, or throw something if they don't let me come. My thoughts are frantic, and every nerve is focused in on my clit, on that buzzing sensation that starts and stops and starts again...but always, it stops.

"Why?" I ask. "Why won't you stop teasing me?"

"We're making it better," Jaxon says, his voice firm. "You need to trust your daddies."

"Do you trust us, Babydoll?" Ryder asks.

My breaths are ragged, but I manage to say, "Yes. I trust you."

Because I do. No matter what hell they're putting me through, I know it's with my pleasure as the goal.

"Beautiful," Jaxon says, cupping my cheek and wiping away my tears of frustration. "Do you think you can handle a little more? Because when you finally come, Babydoll, it's going to be fucking incredible."

"As long as fucking is involved," I say hopefully.

"So much fucking," Ryder says, nodding.

If that's the case, then I can take whatever pleasurable torture they dole out in the interim. Probably.

I'm still sitting on Jaxon's leg. The vibrator is currently off, but now that I've caught my breath and my body is calming down, I expect them to turn it on again at any moment.

"And you can use your safe word at any time," Ryder reminds me.

I shake my head. "I don't want to use my safe word."

His smile is the only warning I get before he turns on the vibrator again. I cling to Jaxon's shoulders, whimpering as my pleasure ratchets higher. And despite the conversation we *just* had, the sensual part of me perks up at the impending orgasm and believes it actually might happen. Maybe this time, *this time*, my daddies will give me some relief.

Jaxon's hands go to my breasts and he fondles them, pinching the nipples. I can't help but writhe against his leg, seeking more sensation, looking for that next thing to catapult me over the edge and into ecstasy.

And then Ryder turns off the fucking vibrator *again*.

"Nooooo!" I wail, mindless in my disappointment, in my frustration. "Please, please, I beg you both, please let me come. I want to come so bad, Daddies. Please."

Ryder pockets the controller and picks me up off of Jaxon's lap, cradling me like a bride. His hands on my skin are hot, melting against me, searing me with their potential for pleasure. I kiss his neck and shoulder and cheek, every part of him I can reach.

"Please, Daddy," I say. "I need to come, please."

"You will," he says. "Just going to let you calm down for a minute, okay?"

I don't want to calm down. I want his cock inside of me now. Jaxon's, too.

Ryder carries me to the living room. He sits down on the couch, still holding me. Jaxon arrives a moment later, lube in hand. I perk up at the sight of it, and both men laugh.

Now that I'm no longer on the verge of an orgasm, Ryder flips on the vibrator again, but he leaves it on the lowest setting. Just enough of a sensation to drive me mad, but not enough to get me off.

"Sadist," I grumble.

He smiles. "Guilty as charged. Sit on my cock, Babydoll."

I scramble to a different position and yank at his pants. He helps me get them down enough that his cock is free, then he pulls off his shirt in one smooth motion. I love watching his abs ripple when he does that. I turn to Jaxon and make a "well, come on" gesture, encouraging him to get naked, too.

His brown eyes darken. "I get to decide when to join in, not you."

If I weren't worried about them withholding another orgasm from me, I would stick out my tongue. But as of now, I think I've endured enough punishment and I'm not going to tempt fate.

"Sorry, Daddy," I say, lowering my gaze.

He smooths his hand over my cheek, then cups my throat. "It's all right, Babydoll. I love you."

"I love you, too."

"You better listen to your other daddy, and get up on his cock now before he loses his patience."

The buzzing sensation against my clit grows in intensity as I slide down over Ryder's thickness.

"Daddy," I gasp, my gaze clashing with his.

Those deep blue eyes are fierce and focused. He holds my hips, keeping me from rising up and down on him like I really want to do.

"Being with you is heaven," he whispers before taking my mouth in a searing kiss.

The sound of clothing being removed comes from behind me, and I glance at Jaxon. His body is beautiful, proud angles, defined muscles. Both of these men are works of art.

Jaxon runs his hand along my spine, then to my waist, where he tugs on the strap of the vibrator.

"I like this toy, Ryder," he says.

"As soon as I saw it, I thought of Olivia," Ryder responds, then increases the speed of the vibrator.

"Shit," I gasp. "I'm going to come—"

Ryder slows it down. "I want us both inside of you when you come, princess."

"Then both of you get in me already," I growl at Jaxon.

He gives me a light spank. "Who's in charge here?"

"My daddies are in charge," I say, but I'm unable to keep the sulk from my voice.

The next spank is harder, and I flinch on Ryder's lap. He swears and thrusts into me. I grin—my punishment also brought reward. But then Ryder cups one of my breasts and pinches the nipple. Hard.

I gasp and squirm.

"Who's in charge here?" Jaxon asks again, his lips against my ear, his beard tickling my neck.

"My daddies are in charge." This time when I say the words, I have the right attitude.

"Good girl," Jaxon says, opening the bottle of lube. He drizzles some over his fingers, then brings it to my ass.

Slippery, a little cold, but the lube heats up quickly as he smears it around. He puts one knee on the edge of the couch next to mine, then lines himself up, his cock head snug against the tight ring of muscle. When he pushes in, I can't help the moan that erupts from my lips. Ryder kisses my cheeks and my neck, his cock unmoving in my pussy while he waits for Jaxon to seat himself.

And then Jaxon begins to thrust into my ass. My head rolls back against his chest and I moan. I feel so full, so alight with pleasure. It shouldn't be possible to feel so much—it's as if every cell is awake, aware, hypercon-scious of where their bodies touch mine. Ryder uses Jaxon's rhythm to time his thrusts in my pussy. These men together are a fucking drug and as the little vibrator on my clit buzzes away, I realize this orgasm is going to be bigger than anything I've experienced before.

One cock pushes in, the other retreats. Then the other thrusts, and the first pulls back. Again, and again, their thrusting mixes with the vibrations against my clit. Jaxon nudges my back, pressing me closer to Ryder. My breasts rub against his chest with every one of their thrusts, and the vibrator nestled against my clit intensifies. Are they messing with the controller? It doesn't look like it—no, it's that I'm sandwiched between them in such a way that the base of Ryder's cock is pushing it against me even harder. I'm enveloped in their heat and in their scents—Jaxon's citrus and leather, Ryder's scent of a pine forest.

Holy shit, this is going to explode me. Already sparks of heat are shooting through my arms and legs. My toes curl and my legs stiffen.

"We've got you, Babydoll," Jaxon whispers in my ear before biting the edge of it.

"Come for us, princess," Ryder says, his blue eyes fixed on mine.

"I—I can't," I gasp.

"You can," Jaxon says, his voice going dark, his breath hot on my neck. He reaches around me and cups my breasts, rubbing the rough pads of his fingers over my nipples.

Ryder thrusts in a way that presses the vibrator harder against me. "Come now, Babydoll."

My body can't help but obey them. The pleasure overtakes me, a surging, overwhelming wave crashing throughout every part of me. I shout in ecstasy and the men tense up, their own orgasms triggered by mine.

"Fuck—Olivia—" Ryder says, surging forward and capturing my lips in a kiss while his cock pulses within me.

Jaxon strokes hard and fast before going still against me, other than his cock, which jerks rhythmically as he comes.

There's nothing more for me to do—I couldn't move if I wanted to. So I let myself fall against Ryder. The vibrator turns off and I murmur a quiet "thank you, Daddies," before my lids close.

I'm barely conscious as Jaxon carries me somewhere. I know it's him holding me because of his citrus scent. The sound of the bathtub running reaches my ears, and then they're taking off the infernal harness and vibrator. They each climb into the tub with me, where they gently wash me up. Before the water can get cool, they help me out. I love the sight of their glistening bodies, all wet and muscular, and if I hadn't just had the orgasm of my life, I might be hinting for another go.

But that'll have to wait until I've slept.

They bundle me in a towel, and next it's Ryder carrying me, his arms strong around me as he walks us to bed and gently sets me beneath the covers Jaxon pulls back. They climb in on either side of me.

"I love you," they each say. Their voices are low and rough, rumbling through me on either side.

"I love you," I whisper, just before I fall asleep, surrounded by my two favorite men in the universe.

～

Olivia

We can't stay at the cabin forever, although I pout at the idea of leaving. Jaxon mentions security being harder when we're here, and I stop pouting immediately. I didn't like inconveniencing the bodyguards before, but now, after Cal, I'm especially sensitive. If making their job easier also means they're safer, then I'll return to San Esteban. The cabin will still be here once all the other trouble is resolved.

And I have to hope that someday the trouble will be resolved. I like my bodyguards, but someday it would be nice to go places without them.

One other aspect crowds to the forefront of our need to leave the idyllic comfort of Ryder's cabin: my mother wants to have that dinner with Jaxon and Ryder and me.

And it's tonight.

Crap.

We're going to meet at her place in Clear Springs. Bodyguards are coming with us, and Mom has hired her own private security, as well. We're being ridiculously cautious, but none of us wants to chance another tragedy.

On our way back from the cabin to San Esteban, my mom is already texting. *Does Ryder or Jaxon have dietary restrictions or food sensitivities?*

Do they both drink wine? Should I have beer on hand as well? I'll provide nonalcoholic options too, of course.

Is red meat okay, or should I make chicken instead?

She's obsessing over this, and her anxiety is sparking my own. After answering all of her questions, I add, *Please relax, Mom. Everything's going to be great.*

At least, it'll be great as long as she was still planning

to be supportive of this relationship. I don't know why I'm worried she'll change her mind and take back her acceptance, because I really don't see that happening. I just want everything to go right.

I want her to like my boyfriends—both of them. And I want them to like her.

First, though, we need to get back to the penthouse and get ready for dinner.

We pull into the parking garage beneath the penthouse and we're getting out of the car when my phone buzzes with yet another text.

"Ugh, my mom's being impossible," I say to Jaxon, checking the texts.

But the text isn't from Mom. It's from Samantha. *Hey, can you come over?*

Sure, how about tomorrow? I write back. *Tonight is the dinner with my mom and the guys.*

Actually, I need you today, she texts. *Like, soon? It's important, or I wouldn't ask. It won't take long, but I really need you.*

What's the emergency? I write back.

Just a conversation.

She's being weird. A conversation is also an emergency? *Is everything okay?*

Yes. Yes, I promise it is. You'll understand when you get here.

I tell her I'll be there in fifteen and look over at Jaxon and Ryder. "I've got a bestie emergency. She said it won't take long. Can I meet you back here before it's time to go?"

"Sure," Jaxon says, but he peeks at the time on his

phone. "We have an hour before we need to leave for Clear Springs."

Cora and Roman get back in the car, and I do too. "Samantha's place?" Roman asks.

"Yeah," I say. "Do you need a break or anything, first?"

"No, we're good," Cora says, offering me a faint smile. "Thanks for asking."

I know these bodyguards are just doing a job, and we'll never be besties, but as we've spent more time together, I've grown fond of them. And I never knew that fondness was reciprocated until Cal's funeral, when we bonded over our sorrow.

Once we get to Samantha's, which is just on the edge of the Bellefleur district, Cora and Roman walk me to the door. Samantha lets us in. They go inside first and stand in the living room, looking intimidating. Samantha looks a little disappointed that Terrence isn't here, but she's also extremely nervous. It's not something the body-guards would notice, but I can tell in the way she starts chattering. She tends to talk a lot, but right now, she's going on and on about her morning and how her room-mates were absolute nightmares and nobody wanted to clean, and that's why the place looks like such a wreck....

"Samantha," I say, interrupting her when she starts an anecdote about the broken dishwasher. "What's going on?"

"Oh, right," she says, widening her eyes at me. "Can you come with me to my room for a sec? I want to show you this dress I'm thinking of wearing to Vice tonight."

This is not an emergency conversation at all. I should be back at the penthouse, picking out my own dress for dinner at my mom's, and nervously checking on Ryder and Jaxon to make sure *they* aren't nervous. They won't be, but that won't stop me from asking them every five minutes. But Samantha made me think this visit with her was really important.

"Please?" she says, as if sensing my reluctance.

Huffing a sigh, I say, "Fine, but you're being weird."

She leads me to the second bedroom down the hall. She goes inside first and I follow her, then she closes the door after me.

"Look, don't be mad," Samantha says. "You're safe. This is just a conversation."

But confusion makes a whirling loop through my body, followed by a sharp stab of anger.

There's a woman standing in Samantha's bedroom.

Genevieve.

5

Olivia

"Please don't be mad," Samantha repeats, and her eyes get shiny with tears.

I'm looking at Genevieve. The woman who tried to ruin the friendship between Jaxon and Ryder. The woman who tried to steal them away from me. The woman who tried to wreck my charity dinner. She's wearing her hair up in a messy ponytail instead of the carefully styled waves I've seen her in before, and her clothes are disheveled. But it's definitely the same woman.

"Oh, *fuck no*," I say, backing up.

"I think you should hear her out, O," Samantha says.

"Are you *serious*?" I hiss at her. "My mom is currently waiting for me to come to a dinner with my *two boyfriends* and *this* is what you're throwing at me now?"

Samantha wipes her water eyes and then glares. "I just made that woman get completely naked in my bedroom so I could make sure she didn't have any weird weapons or wires or some other spy gadgetry bullshit on her, and it was awkward as hell, but we both did it because the two of you need closure. Your mom and your boyfriends can wait two freaking minutes for you to hear what this bitch has to say."

"You tricked me into this," I say.

"Is everything okay in there?" Cora's voice comes from the other side of the door.

I glare back at Samantha. "Is it?"

"It's fine, I promise," Samantha says.

I might be pissed as hell at Samantha right now, but I trust her. With my life, it seems.

"Yes, it's okay," I tell Cora. Once the sound of her footsteps diminishes down the hallway, I point at Samantha. In a quiet voice, I say, "Explain now, or I'm screaming for help."

"Look, I didn't have much of a choice—" Samantha begins.

"I'm sorry," Genevieve says softly, interrupting her. "I begged her to do this. She wouldn't take money, Olivia, and she wouldn't take any kind of bribe. I finally had to resort to explaining my intentions." She gives a little, bitter-sounding laugh. "Funny, how the truth is more effective than money."

I fold my arms across my chest. "And just what are your intentions?"

"I really do want closure," she says. "That's it. Absolution and forgiveness would be nice, but I know I don't deserve those, not yet."

"Then what the hell are you doing here?"

Samantha leans against the wall, looking like she wants to be anywhere else.

"I've been...working on myself," Genevieve says. "I've been seeing a therapist, something I used to refuse to do. Or if I did see one, I'd have him or her all figured out and half in love with me before the first month was over. This latest one called me on it, so I'm listening."

I notice she's not wearing her daytime collar anymore, and that, to me, says more than her words. She also doesn't look as perfect and put-together as she has the other times I've seen her. Her clothes are still expensive and she definitely has a wealthy vibe, but there's something more humble about her now.

Just like my gut told me Nate was bad news, even though we still don't have proof of that, my gut is telling me to hear out what Genevieve has to tell me.

"I've been working on myself, too," I say.

Her voice is so quiet, I almost don't hear what she says next. "I knew Cal, a little. He was a good man."

My throat closes up.

Genevieve looks as if she wants to reach for my hand, but she tightens her own in a fist and leaves it at her side. "I'm sorry—I'm not here to make you cry, I promise," she says.

I can only nod.

"I can do the talking," she continues. "Mostly I want to apologize. I'm crazy about Jax and Ryder. I think I always will be. But I don't need to *be* crazy. The aftermath of your charity dinner was a wake-up call to that. I'm really glad you weren't hurt badly—that was never my intention. I was just so humiliated, and I wanted to take you down with me."

I don't know what to say to that, so I keep quiet.

She goes on, her blue eyes earnest, "So, I think you're very lucky, and I am coming to hope that someday, I might get that kind of luck, and love, again."

"I hope you find it again, too," I say. With someone completely different, of course. She can't have my guys.

Faint winter light comes through the blinds of Samantha's window. It's getting late, and I still have to get ready for dinner tonight.

"Look, I'm sorry, I have to get going," I say.

"Okay. I appreciate your time here. One last thing—consider it a peace offering." She pulls a manila envelope, legal-sized, from the big handbag at her feet. "This isn't my proudest moment. In fact, I'm deeply ashamed. I know Jaxon and Ryder don't trust me, and I deserve that. But if you could give this to them, I would really appreciate it. This may help them with your current problems."

I take the envelope from her. "I don't understand."

"After Cal was killed, I had a private investigator look into it, and he connected the dots to a large company—and I used to date one of that company's board members. There's some info in there that might be of use to you. Don't let anyone except Jaxon and Ryder know you have it, though."

Too curious to wait, I unwind the string holding the envelope closed and peer inside. The large JTS logo is emblazoned on the top of the first paper I see. I look back up at Genevieve, and she nods.

"This means something to you, doesn't it?" she asks quietly.

"Yes, it might." My heart is pounding fast and hard in

my chest. "I don't...I don't know what to think. What's in here?"

"All the information I could wheedle out of my ex." She pushes her hair back behind one of her ears, suddenly looking nervous. "Well, all I could get without sleeping with him again. He was never very good to me, so...I'm sorry I couldn't take it further."

"No," I say, and Samantha shakes her head, too. "It's not worth it. Not for this."

"Well, maybe it is," Genevieve said, "but I just couldn't stomach it. Anyway, there's some papers that might be incriminating evidence in there that my ex didn't realize he was giving me, since he was a bit...distracted at the time."

My stomach gives a little turn, on Genevieve's behalf. I don't know what she did to distract him, and I'd really rather not know.

"I really appreciate this," I say as I stuff the envelope into my handbag, "and your apology, too."

"Thanks," she says with a little shrug. "It's the least I could do. I think I'll stay here until you and your body-guards leave, if that's all right, Samantha?"

Samantha nods. She looks miserable, though, and seems afraid to look me in the face as we leave her room.

Sighing, I stop her in the hallway and reach over to squeeze her hand. "It's going to be okay," I say.

"You're not mad at me?"

"I am a little," I say, "but I can see why you had to keep this quiet and surprise me with it. Still...next time just tell me. I promise I'll listen to you, okay?"

She nods and grabs me in a tight hug. "Okay. Thanks for understanding. Her sob story was too much. I won't ever be friends with her because of what she's done, but I understand so much more now. She's been mistreated left and right. I know she's a master manipulator, but she seems so genuine now."

"Yeah, I know," I say, patting the outside of my bag and making sure the manila envelope is still in there. "I'll see you soon, okay?"

"Yeah. Thanks again, for understanding."

I hug her again. "Always, bestie."

We leave Samantha's, and my steps are fast in my rush to get to the car. I want to look at the envelope. Is there incriminating evidence in here? What does it say? Will it be enough to take down JTS so they'll finally leave me and my mother alone?

But there's no opportunity to look at it now, not unless I want to tell Cora and Roman that I just saw one of our enemies and didn't tell them about it.

And how am I going to tell Jaxon and Ryder? They're going to be so pissed, a part of me wants to not say a word.

I'm definitely going to tell them, but I'm not sure *how* to tell them. They're going to be angry that Genevieve was able to talk to me in person, and that Cora and Roman were there, but unaware of it. I don't want to get my bodyguards in trouble, because I lied to them, too.

Shit, shit, shit.

Ryder

Despite looking nothing like Olivia, Olivia's mother is a lot like her in other ways. Both women are eager to have this dinner go off without a hitch, and they desperately want everyone here to like each other.

No problem with that. The congresswoman, "Call me Faye," is immensely relatable and is genuinely interested and curious about Jaxon's and my lives. Yes, part of that is she's feeling out just how serious we are about her daughter.

Serious as fuck, I want to tell her, but I don't come right out and say it because I'm not that big of an asshole. Plus, she hasn't asked the question aloud.

What's weird, though, is Olivia is acting strange. I don't think it's because we're at dinner with her mom. I've heard the two of them talk on the phone—or at least, I've heard Olivia's end. It's not always great between them, but it's never strained or awkward like Olivia's acting now.

"Before the two of you ran Ironwood, Jaxon and Ryder, what did you do?" Faye asks.

"We started it right out of college," Jaxon answers. "Other than 'student,' my title was 'bartender.'"

Olivia is chewing her bottom lip, barely paying attention.

"I was a stripper," I say,.

Faye's jaw drops, and I chuckle.

"Just kidding," I say.

Olivia barely reacted to the stripper joke. Something is definitely up with her.

Setting aside the problem of her unease for the moment, I continue, "I worked at the university bookstore until graduation. Then, Jaxon had the business idea for Ironwood. We worked a couple nights a week, each, at a club in downtown San Esteban as security, just to get our names out there and keep the lights on in our first office."

Jaxon grins at the memory. "We ate a lot of canned soup in those days."

"It must have been hard to grow from the very start," Faye says.

"It certainly wasn't easy," Jaxon agrees.

We'd gotten our first big break through Genevieve, actually, although we didn't hook up with her right away. Once she hired us, she brought our company to the notice of other wealthy clients. Before long, we landed a couple of solid investors and we were able to expand.

And now we're expanding again. It won't take long for Ironwood to become the premier security agency on the west coast. If we want to put the work in. I'm not sure either of us does, though.

Maybe we'll sell. Or bring in some partners so we're not doing all the work. I know I, for one, want to spend more time with Olivia, less time working. Pretty damn sure Jax feels the same.

Dinner passes with more light chitchat, and then we head into a sitting room for coffee and cookies. Faye isn't bad, actually. There is a faint strain between her and Olivia, but she seems interested in making up. She's asking plenty of questions about the Youth Arts organization, as well as some about Olivia's art projects. What I see here is a mother who has realized she fucked up, and she's making an effort to be better. I hope it works, for Olivia's sake.

It would probably be working better right now if

Olivia wasn't so distractible and uncomfortable. I need to get to the bottom of this. Taking pity on my woman, I wait until nine o'clock and then say, "Hey, we should probably be heading back. I don't want to be on the road too late."

"You're welcome to stay," Faye says, setting down her porcelain cup of decaf coffee. "There are guest rooms, and you're of course welcome to work out whatever sleeping arrangement is best, although I'll warn you, I don't have anything larger than a queen-sized bed."

Olivia blushes beautifully and I can't help sending her a wink when her mother isn't looking.

Jaxon says, "It's kind of you to offer, but I think it's best if we head back to San Esteban. We have the bodyguards to consider, also."

"Of course," Faye says. "I'm so glad you three came for dinner."

"Thank you for having us," I say. "It was a pleasure to get to know you better."

Everything is calm, respectable, drama-free as we leave. Our team of bodyguards get into two other cars which will flank us on our way back to San Esteban.

"All right, Babydoll," I say as soon as the three of us get into Jaxon's car. "Tell me what's really bothering you."

She makes a soft squeaking sound, reaches into her handbag, and pulls out a folded legal-sized envelope.

"I didn't know how to tell you," she says. "I *still* don't know how to tell you."

"Hand it over," I say.

Olivia passes me the envelope. "Are you mad at me?"

6

Jaxon

"I'm not mad at you...yet," Ryder says to Olivia. I start the car while Ryder, sitting in the back seat with her, takes a sheaf of papers from the envelope and begins to look through them.

"Is *this* why you were acting so guilty at dinner?" I ask Olivia, meeting her eyes in the rearview mirror.

"I was acting guilty?" she says.

I nod and pull out of her mother's driveway, onto the road. "Yeah. I thought you were feeling weird about your relationship with us while we were visiting with your mom."

"No, that wasn't it at all," she says. "I have a confession to make, and...you're not going to like it. And I don't want anyone to get in trouble."

"Hold up," Ryder says, eyes on the papers in his hands. "This—wow. This shit is serious. Jax, you need to

drive us straight to the police station. Call your cop friend
—Detective Baldwin."

"What is it?" I ask.

"There's all kinds of evidence in here. Emails.
Meeting notes. Records of payments made, purchases
made. Shit, there's an employee roster, too. Lisa
Albertson is on this list."

Lisa Albertson—the bodyguard who accosted Olivia
in the bathroom and started a massive problem between
the Olivia, Ryder, and me.

"Where did you get this, Olivia? Who is it about?" My
hands tighten on the steering wheel. I'm ready to pull the
fuck over and grab the papers so I can see for myself.

"It's about JTS," Olivia says, her voice small.

I realize I sounded very angry just now, and I don't
want to scare her, so I soften my voice as I ask, "And how
did you come to be in possession of this envelope?"

"That's what I'm afraid to tell you guys," she says.

"The sooner you tell us, the better," I say.

She takes a deep breath. "I don't want Cora or Roman
to get in trouble. They had no idea."

"*Had no idea of what, exactly*?" Ryder asks in a low
voice. He sounds just as furious and anxious as I feel.

Olivia's voice is miserable. "I spoke to Genevieve
today."

"You *what*?" Ryder exclaims.

This is too much. I pull over to the side of the road.
We're out in the middle of nowhere, so once I've parked, I
grab my phone and text the guards to let them know
everything's okay and we're stopping to have a
conversation.

They'll probably think we're fucking—especially

Terrence and Cora, who are in the scene and know what we get into—but I don't care about that. Right now, I only care about Olivia's safety, and why she would take such a foolish risk.

Once that text is taken care of, I look at Olivia through the rearview mirror. Her gaze meets mine briefly before she looks down.

"You're mad," she says.

"Yes," I say. "We gave you bodyguards to prevent things like this. Genevieve could've sent the envelope in the mail, either to us or to the police station. You could've screamed as soon as you saw her. This didn't have to be a secret; it could've happened safely."

"She wanted to apologize to me," Olivia says.

Ryder snorts. "And you believed her?"

Olivia's gray eyes flash with indignation. "Yes, I fucking believed her, and I'm glad I heard her out. She's hurting, you guys. I don't know what she went through before she was with you two, but I don't think everything about her is lies and manipulation. She said that she's going to therapy and from the way she spoke about it, I believe her."

"And then she gave you this mystery envelope," I say, unable to keep the dark skepticism out of my voice.

"Yes, she gave this mystery envelope." Impatience leaks through Olivia's every word.

"Be careful about your tone, little one," I say.

"No," she says. "This isn't anything to do with our dynamic."

"Maybe not, but it has *everything* to do with us protecting you," I say, turning around in my seat so I can face her.

She folds her arms across her chest. "I trusted my instincts and guess what—we ended up with some good information, and Genevieve and I have closure, and you two can just...you can just..."

Under Ryder's and my glares, she trails off.

"I'm going to get spanked so hard, aren't I?" she whispers.

"Eventually," I say. "It's not safe to hang out on the side of the road like this, and I want to get that envelope to the police station ASAP."

Ryder nods. "Good idea. But first..."

He takes out his phone and snaps a photo of every page. He texts each photo to both Olivia and me. It takes a good ten minutes because there are so many pages. Now we all have copies. Overkill? Maybe. But I'd rather be safe than sorry.

Unlike a certain babydoll, who doesn't seem to care about her own safety.

Ryder and I will need to make sure that lesson sinks in for her, later tonight.

I get us back on the road toward San Esteban, and the car ride is full of tension. I'm still angry that Olivia willfully put herself in danger after everything that has happened. While it's great that she trusted her instincts, it's also scary as fuck to know she's doing things like meeting with Genevieve without telling us, or her bodyguards.

Baldwin is waiting outside the station when we arrive. I don't want to pass him the envelope here on the steps, so I follow him inside while Ryder and Olivia wait in the car.

The station isn't quiet, not even this late at night, but he leads me to a quieter area.

"This should have everything you need to know about JTS," I tell him, handing over the envelope.

He nods. "Can't wait to fucking take them down. They're everywhere, and we just needed proof. The FBI is going to want to know about this."

"Good," I say. "I can't wait for this to be over."

Baldwin nods. "Cal was a good man, and Olivia's a sweetheart. I don't like to see all this bad shit happening to her, over and over again."

"Thanks," I say.

"I'll keep you posted," he says, "whatever I can share."

Olivia

Yep, Jaxon and Ryder are pissed. I knew they would be, and dammit, I still have no regrets. It was the right call to talk to Genevieve and I stand by that.

But...maybe I should've let the bodyguards know.

Shit.

Well, just because Jaxon and Ryder have a good point doesn't mean they can be all bossy and tell me what to do.

Except that's exactly how things work with them.

My ass is going to sting later.

Sure enough, once we're back in the penthouse, the elevator door closes and Ryder and Jaxon both face me, their arms folded across their broad chests.

"I know, I fucked up," I blurt.

Jaxon's voice is pensive, but low and growly, and it seems to travel straight to my pussy. "How do you think you fucked up?"

I realize I'm wringing my hands together, so I form fists and move them to my sides. "I don't regret talking to Genevieve. I don't regret accepting the envelope from her."

Ryder nods. "Go on."

"But I should've told Cora and Roman what was happening. There was a point that I could've done that, and I didn't. I didn't want to lose the chance to talk to Genevieve, but that was an excuse, not a real reason." Taking a deep breath, I say, "I'm sorry, Daddies."

Jaxon's brown eyes soften and he takes a step forward, pulling me into his arms. "You're forgiven, Babydoll."

I exhale, then pull in a deep breath of his citrus and leather scent. He feels so safe, secure around me. Wordlessly, I reach for Ryder. He comes over and hugs me as well. His scent reminds me of the forest and of his cabin.

"Do you forgive me, too, Daddy?" I ask, looking at Ryder.

"Of course, princess," he says.

"Does this mean I don't have to get a spanking?" I ask hopefully.

Ryder just smiles and shakes his head. "Sorry, baby girl, but you are *definitely* getting a spanking after the shit you pulled today."

I take my spanking like a good girl. I know I deserve it—both the stinging pain and then the hot lust that follows in its wake. And after the spankings are over, they make me come again and again, reminding me that they're my daddies and all they want to do is take care of me, keep me safe, and give me love and pleasure.

Ryder

One week passes, then another. Jaxon hasn't heard from the detective yet, but based on the things I saw in that envelope, there are more things afoot at JTS than even relates to foxes or the congresswoman or Olivia. It's probably the kind of shit that goes beyond Baldwin's level. Jaxon mentioned the FBI, and if that's the case, we won't be getting any updates.

Olivia now has four bodyguards when she goes out. She's still getting her Youth Arts organization going, with the help of her new hires. The kitchen area of the warehouse is apparently a hot mess, and she's been juggling appointments with contractors and electricians, trying to fix up a hole in the kitchen wall so she can move in a new refrigerator. I know I shouldn't think it's cute when she's swearing under her breath, but it *is* cute.

The people working with her seem nice, and I've met a couple of them. Kathryn is going to be an amazing asset. I'm withholding judgment on the others. Luckily for him, that Nate asshole disappeared. And although his name didn't show up in any of the documents Genevieve gave to Olivia, I have no doubt he's involved with JTS in some way.

I'm sitting on the sofa, scrolling through my phone to browse some of the kinkier offerings from my favorite sex toy store, when the elevator doors slide open and Olivia steps through. Her hair is piled on her head in a messy bun, and she's wearing worn jeans and her old college sweatshirt. Getting-dirty clothes, she called them this morning, because she and a few others would be setting up work spaces in the warehouse.

"Daddy," she exclaims, rushing forward.

I set down my phone and hold out my arms, and she falls into my embrace. I can't believe I used to push this girl away and deny the growing feelings between us. I was a fucking stubborn idiot.

"Did you see the news?" she asks. "No, obviously you haven't, because holy crap, Ryder, you wouldn't believe it —just—pick up your phone and look now."

Not waiting for me to grab the phone, she picks it up instead. Her eyes go wide at the images on the screen.

"Are you looking at porn?" she squeaks.

I laugh. "Nope. I'm shopping."

I wouldn't have thought it possible for her eyes to get even wider, but they do.

"I...I don't want to wear those," she says.

"You never know," I tell her, "they could become your very favorite nipple clamps."

She shakes her head quickly and crosses her arms over her chest, as if the metal teeth of the clamps could magically reach her through the phone. "Nope. Nope-itty-nope-nope."

I close the browser and say, "You said something about the news?"

"Oh! Yes! They raided the homes of several JTS executives."

"The fuck, seriously?" I type in my favorite news site,

my heart thudding with excitement. Just as the site comes up, Jaxon texts Olivia and me.

Check the news, he writes. *I'm coming home now to celebrate.*

Live updates are still coming through for the JTS story, and I press *play* on the video. A reporter stands in front of a mansion where people in FBI jackets enter and exit. We catch her in the middle of a sentence.

"...and they're continuing to carry out boxes of what looks like papers, although it's difficult to get a good view. Marshall, is it the same for you at James Bell's residence?"

"It is indeed, Caroline," a man says as the screen cuts to a different mansion. This place must be in a different time zone, because it's already completely dark. "James Bell was taken out of the residents moments ago, wearing handcuffs. No sign yet of his wife or stepson, although sources say the wife is out of the country..."

Olivia and I watch for a few more minutes, but there really isn't any specific information shared, and that's fine. The most important point here is that JTS is crumbling.

Jaxon arrives just after I've tossed the phone on the coffee table and pulled Olivia into my lap to straddle me. The elevator doors whoosh open while I'm dipping my tongue into her mouth and grabbing her ass with both of my hands, pulling her tight against my lap so the heat of her pussy warms my cock.

Jaxon whistles. "Couldn't wait for me, huh?"

"Can you blame me?" I ask against Olivia's mouth.

"Not in the least," he says.

Olivia laughs. "I can go back to work without an entourage of bodyguards!"

"You still need some," Jaxon reminds her.

"Daniel's still out there," I say.

"Ugh." She leans her head against my shoulder and sighs. "That's a mood-killer."

Grabbing her ass and squeezing her against me again, I say, "Nah, we can get you going again."

She sits up and rocks her hips, creating friction over my cock.

She's a temptation too sweet to resist.

"I need to put my dick in you right fucking now, Baby-doll," I tell her.

"I wouldn't mind that," she says, her voice breathy. She reaches for my pants, but I stop her.

Cupping her throat with my hand, I squeeze a little, just to remind her who's in control.

Then Jax and I get her naked and we celebrate the downfall of JTS the best way we know how.

She's going to feel the effects of our rough love tomorrow, every time she sits down.

Olivia

It's the middle of the night and I'm wide awake. That's what happens when Jaxon and Ryder fuck me into oblivion at six p.m...I go to bed way too early and then I can't sleep.

But after the way they used my body and wrung every drop of pleasure from it? No complaints here.

Also, I could wake them up and they'd do it all over again. Sleep problem solved. But I'm facing Jaxon. In the dim light, I can see the contours of his face. He always looks so stern, but in sleep, he's softer somehow. His handsomeness takes my breath away.

Carefully, I turn around so I can look at Ryder. Yep, just as handsome. My heart gives a happy little leap in my chest. These men are mine. They love me, and I love them.

Whatever weird shit is going on in the outside world, Jaxon and Ryder are my home, and I am happy.

7

Jaxon

Olivia sings in the shower. I grin and hold off on blending our breakfast smoothies so I can listen to her.

There's a book open on the kitchen island in front of Ryder, but he isn't reading it. Instead, he's also listening to Olivia sing.

"What song is that?" he asks.

I shrug. "I don't recognize it."

"You're such an old man," he says with a laugh.

"It's not like you know it, either, asshole."

"At least I recognize the fucking melody," he says. "I think it's a Bastian Crown song."

"Bastian Crown *is* old," I say, throwing a damp dishtowel at him.

We stop bickering to listen to Olivia.

"She's happy," I say.

Ryder's blue eyes are pensive as he says, "Did we help

with that? Or is it more just who she is? Like her inner light or whatever?"

I shrug. "She wasn't happy when we met her, because of her ex. But she still had that...that indefinable quality about her—the thing that just draws me to her, you know?"

"Yeah," he says with a nod. "I know."

"But I haven't seen her this buoyant in a while. I feel like we must've had something to do with it. I hope so, anyway."

"I want her to always feel happy like this," Ryder says.

I do, too.

"You know," he says thoughtfully, "this is going to sound bizarre. But I had this dream, right before we met her. I woke up before I got many details, but when we first danced with her at Vice, I felt like things were falling into place. It pissed me off and scared me, but that's how it felt. Crazy, right?"

Thinking about that time right before we met Olivia, I look over at Ryder in shock. "I had a dream, too. It was her, I'm a hundred percent sure. We were fucking her in the dream, and she loved it."

He laughs. "This is so fucking corny, but Olivia is literally the girl of our dreams."

"Yeah, she is."

The shower water turns off, and she stops singing. I blend up our smoothies and have them in glasses when Olivia pads into the kitchen wearing a robe, the fabric at the neck and shoulders damp from her hair.

Ryder playfully grabs the hem of her robe and lifts it. She smacks his hand away with a giggle, and then he grabs her and tilts her back for a kiss before releasing her.

"Good morning, Babydoll," I say as she walks over to get her smoothie—and a kiss from me. She tastes like minty toothpaste and happiness and holy fuck I am so gone over this girl.

Breakfast is quiet and comfortable. Olivia chatters about her plans for the day, mostly involving setting up the warehouse. "I'm almost ready to open Youth Arts to actual, you know, *youth*," she says with a grin. "We're so close to doing art in that space, I can taste it."

"You're going to change peoples' lives," I say. "I'm so proud of you."

She looks down at the table. "I hope so. I just want to encourage kids, give them opportunities to pursue art when they might feel like it isn't a viable option. Or give them the chance to try out new media..." She trails off and gives a little laugh. "Well, you two have heard me talk about this ad nauseum, so I can stop now."

"I don't mind hearing it again," Ryder says, reaching across the table and taking her hand. "We're both proud of you. Anything we can do to help, let us know."

"I will," she says, grinning at us both. "Thank you."

Standing up, Ryder kisses the top of her head. "I have to get to work."

Olivia stands, too, and pulls his face down for a proper kiss.

He chuckles and tries to pull back. "If you want a good fucking, you're going to have to wait, princess. I scheduled a meeting with our tech team and I can't be late."

Olivia grabs his belt buckle and tugs him back, trying to put her hand into his pants.

He grabs her wrist and holds it behind her along with the other. "Jax, can you give me a hand here? I want to give Babydoll a little lesson in patience."

"Oh, shit," Olivia says. "No, I'm sorry, Daddy."

"You will be," he says darkly, but there's a smile on his face.

I set down my smoothie and stand behind Olivia, where I hold her arms behind her back. Ryder pulls on the belt of her robe, loosening it.

"You're so gorgeous, princess," he says, reaching down and squeezing his dick through his jeans.

My own dick is getting pretty fucking hard. From my place behind her, I can glimpse the swell of her tits. Ryder reaches for her and she gasps. I step to the side so I can watch what he's doing.

His fingers are between her legs. I'm reminded of when the three of us were at Vice, when we first met. At the time, Ryder was behind her, reaching around to finger her while I held her in my arms and kissed her as she came.

Olivia rocks her hips forward, chasing whatever sensations Ryder is doling out. I can't resist nuzzling against her neck, that soft place where it meets her shoulder. She smells so damn good.

Abruptly, Ryder pulls away from her and licks his fingers. "See you later, Babydoll. We'll finish this tonight." His eyes meet mine. "Are you on board with making her wait?"

"Fuck yeah," I say, giving her neck a gentle bite.

Ryder leaves with a wave and a grin.

Olivia sighs, obviously wanting me to know she isn't happy about this plan for the day.

I hug her from behind and say, "Patience is a virtue, Babydoll."

"Noooo," she moans, trying to rub her ass against my cock.

I pull away from her and swat her ass before spinning her around and cupping her breasts, weighing them in my hands. She leans into my touch, so I take my hands away and say, "Go get dressed and go to work. The sooner we all get our shit done today, the sooner we can fall into bed together."

She pouts, but she moves pretty damn fast.

I'll never get enough of this girl.

Olivia

The warehouse is quiet when I arrive, Terrence and Roman right at my sides. Roman is his usual, cheerful self. But I haven't seen Terrence smile since the car attack, when Cal was killed. I don't know what to say to make things better for him. I hope he's talking to someone. My therapist is the best. There's got to be a gentle way to suggest her to him, without making him feel awkward.

It's none of my business, but...also, it kind of is. We were both there. We're both hurting. And he knew Cal better than I did, so it's got to hurt him even more.

I punch in the security code and we step into the warehouse. I set my handbag on a table and look around the dark room, eager to get working. Terrence flicks on the light switch.

None of the lights go on. That's weird. Roman and Terrence exchange a look.

"I'll go look for the fuse box," Roman says.

"Wait," Terrence says, but Roman doesn't hear him. He's already trotting off into the darkness of the warehouse.

I can make out the outlines of the cubicle walls we started setting up yesterday. I'm just about to turn to Terrence to say we should go outside because something feels off. But before I can move, the hairs on the back of my neck lift in alarm. On the furniture and boxes in front of me, shadows play upon shadows.

Terrence jumps behind me, blocking me from whoever is entering the warehouse, and a shot rings out.

I scream and duck. Terrence grabs my arm and drags me toward a set of temporary cubicle walls. They're stacked flat on their sides, but there are enough of them to create a cover for us.

Someone is coming through the open entrance, his face nothing more than a silhouette from the light behind him.

Terrence yanks me down, so I can't see what's happening anymore.

Somewhere farther into the warehouse, Roman gives a shout of alarm, probably to warn us of danger, but the warning comes too late. Footsteps sound as the intruder approaches. Somewhere else, someone must have come in through the back. Maybe they climbed the scaffolding outside, and in through a side window once I'd disarmed the security system?

It doesn't matter how they got in here; what matters is they're here now, and I don't know what's happening to Roman.

"Stay down," Terrence says to me through gritted teeth, his voice no louder than a whisper. "Stay behind me. We're going to the kitchen. Wait for it...."

The kitchen is about fifteen feet behind us, the door obscured by another shipment of cubicle walls.

I want to ask Terrence where the attackers are, how many of them could be here, how this could possibly happen. But I can't even open my mouth to speak, I'm so frozen by fear. Will I even be able to make my way to the kitchen when he says it's time?

But he doesn't leave me the option of staying put. He grabs my arm again and pulls me along with him. His movements are awkward and stilted, maybe because we're crouching low and trying to move silently.

The intruders aren't speaking—not to each other, not to us. I wish I could just close my eyes and then open them again and discover this was all a horrible nightmare. But it's real. This is actually happening, right here and now. And I'm so fucking scared, my heart is pounding loud in my ears, drowning out everything else.

In the kitchen, Terrence tugs me to the side so we're sitting flat against the new refrigerator, which hasn't gotten moved into place yet. The wiring was messed up, and an electrician is scheduled to come next week. There's a gaping hole in the wall, about the size of my torso, full of exposed wires and broken drywall, framed by rotten two-by-fours.

I'd been dismayed at the sight of it, and now I feel

even more exposed for some reason, like someone could be watching from behind the wall.

Then I look down at the floor and see dark liquid pooling around Terrence's leg.

"You've been hurt," I say.

"I just need to tie it off," he says.

It's a lot of blood. I look around for something to tie it with, but there's nothing. He pulls off his belt and wraps it around his thigh.

"Hold this in place," he says. "Tight."

I do as he asks, and he somehow gets it fastened. I'm not paying too close of attention because every second, I'm waiting for people with guns to burst into the kitchen.

It would be so easy to fall apart, to curl into a ball and put my arms over my head and just pray it'll all end quickly, painlessly. Just let it be over fast.

But there's too much to live for. Jaxon. Ryder. This organization that will hopefully touch the lives of hundreds, maybe thousands, of young people and bring art into their futures. My mother and I are improving our relationship and I think we'll get to know each other as adults, and respect each other's chosen professions, given time.

There's so much I want to say to Jaxon and Ryder, so much I want to do with them. Vacations. Conversations. Waking up in the early hours of the day and snuggling while we fall back asleep. I want their hands on my skin, their lips on mine. I want the tenderness I see in their eyes every time we greet each other or say goodbye.

For everything to end now, like this? Shots in the darkness, a faceless evil? I can't stand the thought. I'm not ready to say goodbye.

My heart's breaking at the idea that everything could end now, just because...I don't even know why. Did Daniel recruit friends? Is he behind this? Seems unlikely. Just as unlikely as Genevieve. Maybe I'm an idiot, but I really do believe that she wanted to apologize and go her own way in the world, and find absolution.

That leaves JTS, and they should all be taken care of, right?

"Olivia," a male voice sing-songs from the main part of the warehouse. It sounds like he's moving away from the kitchen. "Where are you?"

I look over at Terrence. His face is tight with pain, but he's pulling his phone from his pocket.

"Can I help?" I whisper, pointing, because Terrence seems reluctant to let go of the makeshift tourniquet on his leg.

He nods and whispers, "I think the phone broke when I fell, but we need to try."

My phone is in my handbag...near the entrance to the warehouse where I set it down after we came in. Shit.

"Olivia," the man calls again.

His voice is familiar, and I wrack my brain, trying to place it.

"Is that Nate?" I whisper to Terrence.

He gives a short nod. "I think so."

"Olivia, where are you?" Nate says. "You can't hide for long. I know this place pretty well and there is no fucking way I'm letting you get away with your happy little life while everything *my* family worked for has gone to shit."

Nate's family? He must be related somehow to the higher-ups at JTS.

There's no sense in trying to piece the mystery

together now. We have to get out of here, or find someone to help us. I work Terrence's phone out of his pocket. Blood makes the plastic slippery, and the screen is shattered. I swipe against it anyway, hoping for the screen to light up, to show some sign of life.

Nothing.

Terrence doesn't say anything, but the bleak expression on his face communicates everything I need to know.

We're fucked.

8

Olivia

No phones, no way to ask for help. My bodyguard has been freaking shot. He's bleeding everywhere and he doesn't look right. I've never seen him so still before. It's as if all of his energy is going to keeping himself awake and alert.

"What do we do?" I ask as quietly as possible. "I probably have a first-aid kit around here somewhere." But it's a phone we need.

"Stay put," he says, his voice soft. "I can't chase you down to protect you."

"I'm not going to make your job harder, don't worry," I say. "We're going to get through this."

It's a miracle the man is sitting upright—there's no way he's going to be able to make a mad, heroic dash and carry me to freedom and deposit me into the waiting arms of my boyfriends.

"Olivia!" Nate shouts. "You can't hide for long, you bitch!"

Terrence and I have got to get out of here. "Come on," I say, tugging on his arm. "We need to find somewhere to go."

He shakes his head. "If you can find a place to hide, and I can't move, then you go without me."

"No fucking way," I say.

"I know you feel bad about Cal," he says gently.

I freeze and stop looking for options of places to hide. Stupid move, but I can't ignore what Terrence is saying now. It's the first time he's mentioned Cal, since the funeral.

"It wasn't your fault." Terrence's dark eyes are fastened on my face.

I take his hand. "It wasn't your fault, either."

"If I'd driven faster...."

"No," I say. "It's only the fault of those asshole criminals who ran us off the road."

He closes his eyes, shakes his head. The man was just shot in the leg, but I have the feeling that the pain in his heart is so much worse. Once we get through this, I'm not dragging my feet any more—I'm giving him the phone number of my therapist. He obviously needs to talk to someone about Cal. I'm happy to talk with Terrence, but I think he needs a professional therapist, someone who can really convince him that Cal's death wasn't his fault. Not even Jaxon or Ryder could convince him of that.

My eyes tear up. I want Jaxon and Ryder so fucking bad right now. They symbolize home, safety, love. So much love.

I must get back to them.

Which means I need to put on my big girl panties and get shit done.

There aren't any weapons in here that I can see. I know from the hours I've spent clearing out the place that there won't be much hidden, either. I threw out the contents of the drawers, including flatware. Not that a butter knife would do much to protect us from a guy wielding a gun, but still. A butter knife would've been better than what I have, which is nothing.

I haven't cleared out the cupboards yet, but from what I recall, they're full of plates and bowls. I won't even find a frying pan to use as a shield, or use to whack someone over the head, Rapunzel-style.

"Do you carry a gun?" I whisper to Terrence.

He shakes his head. He looks on the verge of passing out.

"Stay with me," I whisper. I can't lose him, too. Cal died to save me. Terrence has to live.

"If I go," Terrence says, "it's okay. This is my job. I signed up for this."

"You didn't sign up for death," I say, my voice bitter.

He nods. "No, but I signed up for helping people, risking my life for theirs. Protecting people who need it."

It's not fair. His job shouldn't be the thing that takes his life. My life isn't worth more than his.

Clattering and clanging sounds fill the other parts of the warehouse. Any second, Nate's going to come in here, looking for us. There's got to be a better place to hide than just sitting here against a refrigerator. We're too big for the cupboards, and they're full of the old dishes, anyway. It would make way too much noise to try to get into them even if we could manage to fit inside.

The refrigerator is big, but not big enough for two. I don't want to risk either of us suffocating in it.

There is, however, that hole in the wall where the refrigerator is supposed to go. We might be able to squeeze through and hunker down until Jaxon and Ryder figure out that something's wrong and check things out.

Surely when Terrence and Roman don't check in, Jaxon and Ryder will figure out something's wrong. I hope they call the police, rather than coming here themselves.

I eyeball the hole in the wall. I know I could get through it, although I'll get scraped up in the process. But Terrence is a lot bigger than I am. The man's built like a tank.

I point to the hole and whisper to him, "What do you think about hiding in there? Do you think you can fit?"

He doesn't answer. Heart in my throat, I get up on my knees so I can peer at his face in the dim light. It's hard to tell in the darkness, but I think his brown skin looks pale. He's still breathing, but he's unconscious. Shit, shit, shit. He's lost so much blood. I have to get us both hidden until help comes.

I refuse to let further harm happen to Terrence. If I have to carry him through that hole myself, I'll do it.

First, I need to make sure there's enough room for us in there. Or maybe I can put him in the hole, and I can somehow hide in the cupboards, or climb into the refrigerator and leave it propped open. The very thought of that has my pulse pounding louder in my ears, but I'll do whatever it takes.

My chest feels tight with anxiety, but I force myself onto my knees and I crawl around the edge of the old refrigerator to check out the hole in the wall. It's pitch black beyond, but a glint of something shiny past the old wiring catches my eye.

And then the shiny thing moves.

I gasp and fall back on my ass, but thankfully I don't land on anything loud.

"Olivia," a man's voice says from the hole, very quietly.

And this is a voice from my nightmares, a voice I never wanted to hear again, a voice that should only be making sounds from behind bars. I'm thrust back into that cabin, carried on the stairs, an unwilling captive. This shouldn't be possible.

Yet here he is.

Horrified and shocked, I can only gape at the man in front of me.

Because crouched in the open space past the broken wall, half-hidden by rotten wood and crumbling drywall, is my ex.

Daniel.

∼

Ryder

A potential new client sits in front of me, picking an invisible piece of lint from the edge of his shirtsleeve. Usually it's Jax who meets with these kinds of clients—the super wealthy ones who want to speak to a CEO instead of a regular old intake concierge—because he has the patience to deal with their bullshit, and I don't.

But Jaxon's already dealing with a board of investors to discuss of our expansion, and I don't have the patience for that, either.

So here I am with Marco Ruberetta, trying to hype up Ironwood. He's already sold on the security firm, and we're just going through the motions. I think it soothes the ego of a guy like this to have a company court his patronage.

It's nauseating.

The only thing getting me through this day is knowing that I'll get to have sweet, candy-scented sex with my babydoll, Olivia, at the end of it. I can't wait to grab her lush ass, suck on her gorgeous tits, and look into her eyes while she comes.

"You said I won't have a team assigned to me at all times?" Ruberetta asks, his voice bordering on a whine.

Annoyed, I pretend to look over the paperwork in front of me. I'd much rather think about Olivia than deal with this asshole.

"Not necessarily," I say. "Our team will do a threat assessment. It may be that during mundane outings, you'll have a single personal security guard, and during higher-profile events, you may have more. It's completely dependent upon the situation."

"What if I *want* more bodyguards at all times?" he asks.

He's not scared; he just wants the appearance of importance. Yawn. I want to tell him to take his self-importance and shove it up his ass, but Jaxon will get pissy if I send yet another potential client out of here fuming because I've offended them with my blunt treatment.

"There are arrangements we could make, for that possibility," I say, sneaking a glance at the clock on the wall. This meeting has lasted twenty-three minutes, to accomplish nothing other than ego-stroking. "They'll be beyond the constraints our standard protective service contracts, but Ironwood is open to discussing those possibilities with you."

He considers me for a long moment. I feel like I've done a fairly good job disguising my disdain for the guy, but Olivia would probably say I'm still not being polite enough.

I miss her. I should've skipped out on this and gone to the warehouse with her. I bet I could find a room with a chair where I could sit down and let her ride me.

Finally Ruberetta nods, reaches out to shake my hand. I take his oily flesh in mine and shake, while attempting to keep my shudder to myself.

Just as our fingers part, my phone buzzes three times in rapid succession, twice slowly.

Fuck. It's the Ironwood emergency rhythm. Shit's going down with one of our clients, and the team needs me and Jax.

"I'm sorry, I have to take this immediately," I say, reaching for my phone and standing up, hoping to usher him to the door.

Ruberetta's eyes bulge with indignation. "But I just remembered, I wanted to talk about the size of my guards."

The *size* of his guards...what? He wants the biggest

guys so he can look even *more* important? I don't have fucking time for this bullshit.

"We'll have to discuss it later," I say, looking at my phone screen but not comprehending it yet, because this asshole is distracting me. "This is an emergency."

"I am here because I'm a top client," he says, as if I need reminding about his status.

I'm ready to beat this guy up myself, fuck all thoughts of personal security. Now I know why he wants body-guards so bad—he's such a total asshole, he risks getting his face rearranged every time he leaves his house. It's a hazard of being Marco Ruberetta.

"It's an emergency," I repeat, looking down at my phone.

Then I see Olivia's name in the alert text and it's like a massive log has just slammed into my gut, ripping away my breath, stealing my thoughts.

Ruberetta waves his hand imperiously. "The size of guards is more important than whatever..."

His face goes white and he trails off at the look of pure hatred I'm projecting.

"It's time for you to go," I grit through my teeth. "As I said, this is an *emergency*."

"I'll just...see myself out," he says, finally standing and moving to leave.

"You do that. We'll be in touch."

My phone buzzes with a text from Jaxon, but I can't focus to read it. I can't focus on anything. Olivia is in trouble, and I have to find Jaxon and we need to get to the warehouse immediately.

Ruberetta finally leaves, looking distinctly annoyed that he isn't important enough to hold my attention. But nobody else, *nothing* else can hold my attention when Olivia might be in danger.

All I can think of is the text on my phone, coming from our communications team, which alerts us to any anomalies or alarms for our clients.

Roman and Terrence not in contact. Olivia not responding.

9

Olivia

aniel doesn't move toward me. He doesn't reach out to grab me. He doesn't look at all interested in pursuing me in any way.

But my logic doesn't pay attention to these visual cues, and instead snags on the issue that my abusive ex, who once kidnapped me, is right here.

I gasp and scramble away, trying to tug Terrence's limp, unconscious weight along with me, out of the kitchen, and back toward Nate.

I stop before I get very far—partly because Terrence is too big and heavy for me to drag, and partly because I realize I'd rather face Daniel than get shot by Nate.

This isn't fucking fair. None of it is.

"I'm not going to hurt you," Daniel whispers, sticking his face out of the hole so I can see him better. His expression is serious, intent. Whether or not he's telling the truth, I believe he believes this, that he isn't going to hurt me.

"Then why...why are you here?" I ask.

He gives me a weird smile. "I've been looking out for you. I saved you from the fire, too."

"Looking out for me, or stalking me?" I ask.

"Tomato, to-mah-to," he says, with that same, stupid grin on his face.

A loud clatter echoes and bangs in the other section of the warehouse.

"Fuck, Olivia, where the fuck are you hiding?" Nate shouts.

Nate's going to think of the kitchen any second. There are other side rooms, and many other places to hide, but either Nate will think of this room himself, or someone with him will.

"Come on," Daniel says, gesturing me toward him. "I can get you out of this."

I shake my head. Daniel is terrifying. And there's a chance Nate won't kill me. Maybe Nate will just want to talk about how horrible things have been for his family, and I can keep him talking long enough for help to arrive.

Yeah, right. As much as I'd like to think Nate just wants to talk, I know that isn't the case. The bullet in Terrence's leg is clear enough on what Nate's intentions are.

Daniel, or Nate? It's just like that old saying that my mom trots out when she's talking about dealing with politicians and making tough choices—I'm between the devil and the deep blue sea.

"Listen to me," Daniel whispers. "You can get out this way. There's a tunnel."

"What? There can't be a tunnel here."

He gives me a weird look. "It must have been put in several decades ago, to allow flood relief from the reservoir. I've been using the tunnel to get in here and watch over you."

"Watch over me?" This is so creepy. "But you were…"

"Obsessed. I guess that comes along with it," he says, and I can make out his shrug in the darkness. "I can't let them hurt you."

"But *you* would've hurt me."

"I never really wanted to hurt you."

I don't believe it for a second. But maybe, in his sick mind, that's what *he* believes? And he did save me from the fire.

"Can we both get through that tunnel?" I ask, gesturing toward Terrence.

"Leave him behind," Daniel says.

"No way." I shake my head for emphasis.

Daniel's voice is harsh. "They don't care about him—they want you. Come on, Olivia."

I don't understand it, I don't understand why he's here, encouraging me.

He must know, like I do, that remaining here in this kitchen is a death sentence waiting to happen.

But no fucking way am I abandoning Terrence.

"Help me with him," I say, pointing to my bodyguard.

Daniel sighs. "This is stupid."

And there's the ex I remember, diminishing me and telling me that my ideas are dumb.

"It's *not* stupid," I say, "and I'm smart, so stop trying to make me think otherwise. Help me with Terrence or you can just go…go fuck yourself."

Sighing heavily, Daniel heaves himself through the hole. He looks gaunt, like he hasn't been eating well. I wonder if he's been living on the streets. That would make it easier for him to follow me around. People aren't going to notice someone who looks down on their luck, not in this area. And he has the resources to clean himself up when necessary, I suspect.

He approaches quickly, and I struggle not to shy away from him. I need his help, and he's offering it. What this will mean for me afterward, no idea. But at least Terrence will have a chance of getting out of this building and receiving the medical attention he needs.

Daniel grabs one of Terrence's arms, and I take the other. Together, we start to drag him toward the wall.

Footsteps sound outside the kitchen, and we both freeze. Daniel's expression is just as frightened as mine, and before I can say a word, he scuttles away, back into the hole in the wall like the cockroach he is.

No sooner is Daniel hidden than Nate bursts into the room.

I'm too scared to react—I don't even make a sound.

There's nowhere to run, not unless I want to abandon Terrence and follow Daniel through a tunnel to who-knows-where.

A satisfied look washes over Nate's angry expression. "There you are."

Jaxon

Ryder meets me at the elevator and we ride down to the parking garage together. The world is awash in shades of black and red. I'm furious, and I'm fucking terrified that something terrible is happening and I'm not there to do one fucking thing about it.

Neither of us says a word. There's nothing to say. We've done everything possible to protect her, and it still hasn't been enough. Things had seemed safe enough at the time, but maybe we shouldn't have let down our guard once JTS's higher-ups got what was coming to them.

Maybe we should've kept her in my penthouse and never let her out.

Yeah, it's a nice idea from the standpoint of wanting to keep her safe, but not at the cost of her freedom and her ability to live her life. I'm not really a monster, not like that.

But fuck if I don't wish I could keep her somewhere totally safe from harm.

"Police have been notified," I say as we get into my car.

He gives a short nod. "Do you know what intel we have, if any?"

"Leonie and Lin are working on it," I say. "Call them, have them report as we drive."

He jabs some buttons on his phone, then puts it on speaker. After reciting his security number, Leonie says, "Ryder, hey. We're reviewing security footage. It looks like they were separated, the lights knocked out."

"How many are there?" he asks, his voice tight.

"There are three men," Leonie says. "Hell. A shot was fired. It got Terrence in the leg."

"Share that info with the police," Ryder says. "Give them whatever intel we have."

"Lin's with the dispatcher now," she says, and relays instructions to Lin.

Leonie goes on to tell us that she can't see the location of the intruders, but at one point, two of them attacked Roman while the third shot Terrence. Terrence protected Olivia and dragged her somewhere out of the camera's angle.

"I'm not a hundred percent certain," Leonie says, "but I think the third guy, the shooter, is Nate Boyd."

We fucking knew he was bad news.

Caro Boulevard is little more than a blur, and I barely register the change in buildings when we reach the Bellefleur District. The only thing in my mind is getting to Olivia as fast as possible.

Finally, we reach the warehouse. I pull in, tires skidding on gravel as I brake abruptly. There are no emergency vehicles in sight, but the wail of sirens in the distance reaches my ears. Of course we beat the police in getting here. I bet they don't respond as quickly in the Bellefleur District. It would've taken seconds in Dorado Heights. Shit needs to change here.

"The police dispatcher says under no circumstances are you to enter the building." Leonie's voice is firm.

"Got it," I say to her, then hang up and yank my keys from the ignition, preparing to get out of the car.

Ryder glances over at me while he unbuckles his seatbelt. "I'm not fucking waiting for the police."

"Neither am I."

Ryder

The warehouse appears normal, and it's quiet from the outside. The Ironwood car Olivia uses, driven by her bodyguards, is parked neatly next to the front entrance. From this perspective, nothing is amiss.

Terrence is with Olivia, I remind myself. He was shot, but not so badly that he couldn't get her away from the shooter. Roman is down. The last Leonie could see of Roman, he was on the ground.

Fuck. I need them to all be okay.

Jaxon and I hurry to the door. It's slightly open, not open enough that we could've noticed from the street, but up close we can tell. We stand on either side of it and I nudge the opening wider with my foot and wait to see what happens.

No reaction from within.

I ease inside. The entire place is dark. The lights were taken out, from what Leonie could figure. I hate the idea of us going in blind, but there's nothing to be done about that.

Jax and I move to the back, where we know Roman was knocked down. I keep my attention on our surroundings, seeking Olivia in the darkness and shadows, and I know Jaxon's doing the same. Terrence could have brought her to the shadowy areas of any of these large shipment boxes. Many of them have been knocked over, along with the cubicle walls Olivia ordered to separate work areas within the warehouse. This would've been the perfect sort of place to hide her.

But from the tumbled boxes and crates, it appears Nate has already searched this section.

I'm about to turn around and look elsewhere, when a low moan of pain reaches my ears. Jaxon points to the ground near a stack of empty pallets. There, a man's foot and lower leg is visible.

Slowly, we come around the pallets, one of us on either side.

The prone form belongs to Roman. He's fighting to open his eyes, struggling to wake up.

"It's okay," Jaxon tells him. "We're here. Stay down, stay quiet, okay?"

Roman takes a shaky breath and whispers, "Two at least. Possibly three. No more than that. One has a gun. The other two, I don't know."

"Where are you hurt?" Jaxon asks him.

"Bump to the head, hurts like fuck," he says. "Otherwise okay except I fucked up, didn't protect your girl. I'm fucking useless."

"You're still a great bodyguard," I tell him. "We all fuck up sometimes. Stay still, right here."

"Will do," he says, but he looks miserable.

He's so quiet I almost don't hear him when he says, "Two. By the side door, at your six."

I slowly spin around so I'm facing the side door. Sure enough, two guys are wearing black fatigues and sneaking along the edge of the room. They haven't seen us yet. Jaxon scoots forward and nods at me, gesturing that we should again split up and go around them.

Slow, even breaths. I make sure to walk quietly, heel to toe. No stupid mistakes. Fuck, it's been a long time since I did any field training. We make all of our recruits go through it. Jaxon and I have both done it as well, multiple times, but the trainings are held a few miles north of Clear Springs, and I haven't been there in a while.

That'll change, after this.

Jaxon and I are in sync, though, and we reach the guys at the same time. The temptation to snap their fucking necks is strong, but I'm not a killer, never have been. Still, the crunch of my guy's nose against my knuckles is satisfying as hell, and I spot a broken pipe nearby and grab it to hit him in the side of the head. Not too much force; I just need to knock him out.

Down he goes, at the same time as the guy Jaxon grabbed. But when Jax's guy falls, he lands against a stack of crates and the whole thing tumbles, making a huge crashing sound.

Dammit, now every soul in this building will know something's up.

"Do you see any rope or something we can tie these guys with?" Jaxon asks.

I look through the rubble of the crates and find some bungee cords. They're in bad shape, but they'll do for now. Hopefully the guys won't wake up for a while.

We tie them up and search them for guns. They aren't carrying, and that might be the only reason Roman is alive.

A soft gasp sounds in the darkness behind me. Jaxon and I spin around at the same time.

There she is—Olivia. Only she's not alone. I recognize that asshole from photos and profiles gleaned by our tech division. Nate Boyd, just like Leonie thought. He's standing just behind Olivia, and he's got one arm wrapped across her torso. He holds a gun with his other hand, and he's pointing it right at Olivia's head.

10

Jaxon

"**I**f you harm one fucking hair on her head," Ryder warns.

Nate sneers. "I don't think you're in the position for making bargains or threats right now, motherfucker."

Olivia looks terrified. She holds onto Nate's arm, but it's more for balance than any attempt to get away. I try to signal her with my eyes that we're going to get her out of this. *It's going to turn out okay, Babydoll*, I want to whisper. *You're going to be fine.*

"Please, Nate," she says, "let me go. Whatever's going on, we can work it out—"

"Shut the *fuck* up, you stupid bitch," he says. "It's because of you that my family is losing everything. It's because of you that my mom's going to prison."

"Maybe we can work something out," I say, just to

keep him talking. I want the police here. They're trained for this, and they have weapons, tactics.

Then again, their arrival might startle Nate into shooting.

Shit, I can't strategize. I can't logic my way into figuring out what's the best call here. Not when Olivia's life hangs in the balance.

"We can give you money," I say. "Set you up in comfort, even in luxury, for life."

"It doesn't matter!" he screams, spittle flying from his mouth. "My parents will be in prison! The only reason I wasn't rounded up with the rest of them is I don't share their last names—I'm the unwanted stepson who never 'amounted to anything.' They wouldn't even put me on their payroll." He shakes his head. "Sure came in handy when they wanted a spy, but look where it got me. I'm just as much of a loner as I was before."

If he's so lonely that he wants to join his family in prison, he's definitely on track for that.

He shakes Olivia. "And it's your fucking fault, bitch!"

She makes a surprised sound of pain as he jams the gun against her head even harder.

"Please," she whispers, a tear catching on her eyelashes. "Please let me go, Nate. I'm so sorry about your family. Let us try to help you."

Movement behind him catches my eye. Terrence? We sure as hell could use his help about now.

But it isn't Terrence—this guy is smaller, and he has none of Terrence's stealth. His shoes make a scuffing sound on the concrete floor.

Surprised, Nate spins around just as the guy comes flying at him and Olivia.

Nate loses his grip on the gun, and it clatters to the floor. Olivia is quick enough to kick it even as she, Nate, and the third guy tumble to the ground. The gun slides away, behind them and out of our reach.

The new guy and Nate grapple. Olivia takes a fist to the face, and it splits her lip. She tries to crawl out from under the other guys, but Nate grabs her ankle and pulls her back. She slides against the concrete and winces. Ryder and I rush over. Ryder reaches her first and he pulls her away from the flying fists.

Ryder thrusts Olivia at me, then he's diving back into the fight.

"Ryder!" Olivia screams.

I hold her tightly, so grateful she isn't hurt. "He'll be fine, Babydoll, don't worry. We have you now. Everything's going to be okay."

Her breathing is labored as she gasps for air. "No, Terrence is hurt. I don't know about Roman—"

"We'll get them soon, okay?"

The door to the warehouse bangs open.

"Freeze! Police!" a deep, loud voice calls.

Ryder stops fighting immediately and sits back from Nate and the other guy. With the light pouring in through the open door, I can get a better look at them both, and I recognize the other guy's dark hair and pointed nose.

"Is that *Daniel*?" I ask Olivia.

She just nods and holds tightly to my waist.

The police are swarming and they shout command after command at Nate and Daniel as they surround us all.

Nate and Daniel's fight has brought them closer to the gun Olivia kicked away.

Nate inches to the side, his hand outstretched. He grabs the gun.

"Look out, the gun!" Olivia screams.

"Freeze, lower your weapon!" a police officer shouts.

Daniel tries to grab Nate's arm, to squeeze him so Nate has to drop the gun, but in a burst of adrenaline-fueled strength, Nate brings the gun around. He pulls the trigger just as a police officer lets loose another bullet.

Lying across Nate, Daniel takes Nate's bullet. The officer's shot hits Nate in the side of the chest. Right through the heart. Nate slumps to the ground.

I can't see where Daniel was shot, and officers are all over the place, blocking my view. They start to pull Olivia away from me, but she grips me tighter and sobs, so they let her be. I wrap my arms around her and kiss the top of her head, murmuring nonsense words and sounds, trying to comfort her even while the officers roughly grab Ryder and take him off to the side for questioning.

"There are four injured men in here," I tell the nearest officer. "One is back by those stacked pallets. And two are about ten yards that way, tied up near the wall. Olivia, baby, where's Terrence?"

"He's in the kitchen," she says, pulling away from me just enough to point.

EMTs join the chaos, and they lead Olivia and me from the warehouse into the cold November air. She shivers in my arms, but I think it's due more to shock than anything else. An EMT gives her a blanket, which I wrap tightly around her shoulders, and we follow the woman to an open ambulance. Olivia leans against me while the EMT checks out her lip and dabs some antiseptic on that and on her hands, which got scraped when Nate dragged her along the concrete floor.

Moments later, Terrence is brought outside on a stretcher. He's awake, but he looks disoriented.

"Is he going to be okay?" Olivia asks, her hand to her chest as if she's trying to soothe her anxiety.

"I'm sure he will be," I say. "Roman, too."

Roman and the other guys are brought out on stretchers, too, and sirens wail as all of the ambulances head off toward the hospital.

"Babydoll," I say. "Look at me. Are *you* going to be okay?"

≈

Olivia

At first I'm not sure how to answer Jaxon. I can't believe what just happened, what I just saw.

Daniel's dead. They haven't brought him out on a stretcher, and they haven't brought out Nate.

I can't be happy that anyone has been killed, and yet a part of me thinks, just maybe, I'll be free now. Free to live without fear. Free to go places without an entourage of bodyguards. Free to make choices without needing to consider whether the decision may or may not put me in extra danger.

Jaxon's still looking carefully at me, concern in his gorgeous brown eyes. His beard is scratchy-soft beneath my palms as I cup his face in my hands and stand on my tiptoes. I kiss him with the side of my mouth that isn't stinging from the EMT's antiseptic.

"I'm going to be okay," I whisper. "I've got you, and Ryder. Everything will be okay if I have my daddies."

We don't get to leave right away, of course. There are statements to give, thousands of questions to answer. It takes a long time for the officers to release Ryder and stop treating him like a suspect. The fact he's been swearing at everyone and threatening to lose his shit if he doesn't get to hold me isn't earning him any brownie points, that's for sure. I would laugh if I didn't want to hug him so damn badly.

Finally they let him come to me. Jaxon lets me go so Ryder can give me one of the tightest hugs I've ever received. He kisses both of my cheeks, my nose, my neck, and then finally, oh-so-carefully, my lips.

"We'll get to go home soon, Babydoll," he whispers.

It takes forever, but they finally do let us go.

I'm going to sleep for a week.

Olivia

I don't, in fact, sleep for a week, although I do go to bed early, with Ryder and Jaxon on either side of me.

In the middle of the night, I jerk awake. I dreamed of gunshots and blood.

Jaxon's hand is warm against my shoulder and he gently soothes me. "It's okay, Olivia. You're safe, little one."

I sigh and start to relax before tensing up again. "How are Roman and Terrence?"

"They're doing well," Ryder rumbles from my other

side. "I checked in with the hospital an hour ago. We can visit them in the morning, if you want to."

"I want to," I say.

He leans into me to kiss my cheek, and his hard length presses against my hip through his boxer briefs. I reach for him instinctively, sliding my hand along his shaft.

"Olivia," he groans. "You don't know what you do to me."

Jaxon kisses my shoulder and along my throat, his beard tickling my skin. Then he travels lower, lifting up my top so he can kiss the valley between my breasts.

"Is this what you want, Babydoll?" he whispers.

"Yes, Daddy. Daddies. Please," I say.

So much happened today. I haven't even begun to process it all. But what I do know is that these men came through for me. They were there as soon as they could possibly get there, and they've done everything they can to protect me at every turn.

Beyond all of that, they love me, and I love them. These are two very different individuals and yet the adoration I feel for each of them is at the same level. I can't live without them, and the desperation I felt today when I thought I might never get to touch them again, kiss them again—it was so extreme. I need to touch and kiss them now and remind myself that we're all here together, we're alive.

"I need you," I gasp, as Jaxon takes one of my nipples in his mouth and sucks hard, swirling his tongue over the nub.

Clothes slide against skin as my men get me naked. Ryder holds my arms above my head and joins Jaxon in kissing and licking my breasts, each man at a nipple. Their hands travel everywhere else, eliciting fiery sensations of lust. They reach my pussy at the same time and then their fingers are there, sliding through my wetness.

They both push a finger inside me at the same time. I moan and grab blindly at one of them. It's Jaxon. I drag his head back to mine so I can kiss him, and while I do, Ryder trails kisses down my stomach and over my mound, until he's tasting my pussy.

It feels so good, I'm shaking and I can't seem to stop. Jaxon's tongue slides against mine, while Ryder's tongue swirls around my clit. My need and pleasure climb, white-hot and indescribable as they coalesce into a brutal, divine orgasm that leaves me gasping.

I tug on Ryder's shoulders, bringing him up to my other side.

"What do you need, princess?" he asks.

In response, I shove down his boxers and grip his cock. I swing my leg over his hips and take him inside of me. He groans in pleasure and clamps his hands on my hips. I don't move, instead savoring him even while I reach for Jaxon's hand. I guide his hand to my ass. "Take me there, Daddy," I whisper.

"I can't," he says.

"What? Why not?" I ask.

"I can't be gentle tonight." His voice is gruff, dark.

"I don't want gentle," I say, leaning over so I can kiss him.

Ryder's cock twitches within me.

"I don't want gentle," I repeat. "Daddy, I want *you*."

Jaxon grabs my throat, thrusts his tongue between my lips. There's a burst of pain as he bumps against the bruise on my mouth, but I relish the pain because I know he isn't treating me like something fragile. My body is theirs—theirs to pleasure, theirs to punish.

With a groan, he pulls back from my lips and reaches for the nightstand. He's back with a bottle of lube, and then he's moving behind me.

Ryder pumps into me, a growl tearing itself from his lips and his blue eyes black in the darkness of the bedroom, intent on my face. "Your pussy feels so good," he says.

Tremors build within me as Jaxon slides a slick finger against my asshole and presses in. Despite his fear that he can't be gentle, he's still stretching me, making sure I'll be ready for him, and my heart aches with tender happiness.

His cock replaces his finger and I take a deep breath at the inexorable, inescapable sensation of pressure as he begins his slow penetration. I drop my head back and he kisses my neck.

"Here it comes," he whispers, then slams the rest of the way inside of me.

I cry out at the delicious, uncomfortable fullness. Both of my men in me at once. Pleasure for all three of us at once. We're joined together. And as they begin to move, the pleasure only heightens.

"Do you like how your daddies fill you up?" Ryder asks, bringing his hand up to gently hold my neck.

I love it when he does that with my throat. "Yes, Daddy," I gasp.

"You're so wet," he says, pumping in time with Jaxon. "You get wetter when I choke you, Babydoll. You like that, too?"

"Yes, Daddy."

Jaxon has one hand braced on my hip, and he brings the other around to my breasts. Sharp pain travels down to my clit, which rubs against Ryder's pelvis as the men rock me between them.

My heart thuds in the same rhythm as my building orgasm. Fuck, this climax is going to be huge. It always is with them, but this one is even more momentous than the others I've had. Ryder tightens his grip on my throat. My arms shake as I hold my weight. I experiment with rolling my hips, and each man swears in approval.

"Such a good Babydoll," Jaxon murmurs. "You move so well on my cock with your tight, sweet ass."

"Good girl," Ryder says, squeezing my throat and staring directly into my eyes. "Your pussy is heaven, and your heart is ours."

"Yes, Daddy," I gasp. "Everything is for you both."

Ryder's cock pistons faster within me, and Jaxon speeds his thrusts, as well. I'm awash in the sensation and heat of their love, of the heightening friction, the climb toward ecstasy.

"Come for us now, sweetheart," Jaxon grunts, his bearded cheek pressed to my shoulder. "Now, Babydoll."

So I do, shattering between them, held in place by their thick cocks, their warm hands, the open-mouthed kisses they press to my chest and shoulder. Their own frantic thrusting stops and their cocks pulse in place as they come, too.

"Fuck, I love you, little girl," Jaxon breathes against my neck.

"I love you, too, Daddy," I whisper, kissing his

whiskery cheek. Then I turn back to Ryder and kiss him, as well. "I love both of my daddies."

"I love you, too, Olivia," Ryder says, cupping my cheek.

They both clean me up, their movements gentle and attentive, and then we fall back into sleep again. And this time, nightmares don't disturb my rest. They wouldn't dare, not when I'm surrounded by so much love.

11

Ryder

"Olivia," I say through the bathroom door, "if you don't get your sweet little ass out of there immediately, I'm coming in after you."

"Shh, Ryder, someone will hear you," she admonishes.

"Everyone left," I say, looking around the Youth Arts building. "We're alone, Babydoll. It's just you and me here. And if I have to take you over my knee and spank you, well, that'll only make me happy. So you decide how long you want to dawdle."

It's been two months since everything went down at the warehouse. I was concerned about Olivia continuing to use the location after everything that happened, but she's transformed the place. The few times I've gone to see her there, I wasn't even thinking about Nate or Daniel or anything else. It's the kind of place that I would want to settle in and create something magical.

"This dress is so much shorter than my other one," she grumbles, stepping out of the bathroom.

I can only stare. This girl takes my fucking breath away. And her black dress *is* much shorter than the one she wore when we first met.

"Turn around," I say, my voice a low growl.

Her gray eyes widen and she complies, spinning until I'm looking at her back.

"Bend over," I say.

"Ryder..." she says, drawing out my name.

"Fucking do it, princess."

She bends over, slowly, and her hem moves higher and higher up her thighs. When she's fully bent over, I'm treated to a view of paradise—her sweet cunt covered by a tiny scrap of lacy black panties.

"Tsk, tsk," I say. "What would Jaxon say about these very grown-up panties on our little babydoll?"

"I don't think he would like them," she mumbles.

"No, he wouldn't. But I do. Stay put."

I trace her folds through the thin material and inhale deeply. Her arousal still smells like candy to me, and I don't know how she manages that, but fuck if it doesn't turn me on. I'm so damn hard, I feel like one wrong move and I'll be coming in my pants.

She wiggles her ass, trying to get more of my hand on her, and I give her a spank.

She shrieks in surprise, but as I smooth my hand over the sting, she begins to moan.

"Daddy, please," she says. "Could you take me right now? Just a quickie? Please?"

"You beg so beautifully, but no," I say. "Jax and I have plans for you, and it's time we got going. Hold still."

Her legs quiver as she keeps her position. I pull out my phone and snap a photo, then send it to Jaxon. Then I slide her panties to the side and push my finger into her hot, tight pussy. Damn, I wish I could pound into her right now, give her a good taste of what's coming later. Her inner walls tighten on my finger as she tries to take me farther in.

"Time to go, Babydoll," I say, removing my finger. Then I grip the waistband of her panties and tug, tearing them off of her.

"Ryder! I like this pair!"

"*Liked*. Past tense. I'll get you a new pair if you really want them." I grin. "It'll be fun watching Jaxon spank your ass every time you try to wear them."

"Daddy, are you going to tell Jaxon?"

I hold up my phone and show her the picture I snapped. "Already did."

"Ugh. I'm going to be in trouble."

"Yep. I'll keep these tonight," I say cheerfully, jamming the lace into my pocket. My hand bumps against the hard shaft of my dick, and I will myself to calm down.

Tonight's going to be fucking fun.

Emphasis on the fucking.

Jaxon

I'm looking at the text Ryder sent when he and Olivia walk up to the entrance of Vice. Olivia's beautiful pussy, encased in a pair of very adult panties.

"Hand them over," I say to Olivia, crowding her toward the wall so she'll be out of sight of bystanders. Ryder will come over in a second and help block her from anyone else's view. "Right now, little girl. You shouldn't have worn such grown-up panties."

She sighs and looks at Ryder.

"Well?" I say, holding my hand toward her, palm up, waiting. "Take them off and give them to me."

Her pink lips make a little pout. "I can't."

I get up close, gripping her shoulder and sliding my cheek against hers. "And why the fuck not, Babydoll?"

"Because Ryder already took them." She sighs. "He knew you would disapprove of them."

"And you knew it too, sweetheart. You think I don't know what kind of game you're playing with us?"

She blinks up at me, staring at me through her eyelashes, all wide-eyed innocence. "What do you mean, Daddy?"

I'm tempted to throw her over my shoulder and carry her up to the private VIP room Ryder and I booked. But that's for later. Instead, I reach for her bare thigh and travel my hand up beneath the hem until I gripping her bare ass beneath her dress.

"Good call on taking the panties," I say to Ryder. "Easier access."

He shrugs. "Just doing us all a favor."

"I hope it wasn't too much of a hardship," I say with a laugh.

"Oh, it was a huge hardship." His eyes glint with amusement. "But Babydoll will help me out with that later."

Recognizing me, the bouncer lets us in immediately.

The warm interior of the club washes over us, along with the hypnotic, thumping bass of the music. I recognize a song by Bastian Crown, only it's a slow, sexy remix.

Olivia grabs our hands and we go straight to the dance floor, bypassing the bar entirely.

Look at me, say my name
Give me your all
Your submission, my bliss
Lift up your skirt, princess
Give Daddy a kiss.

"These lyrics!" Olivia says, a smile on her face. "It's like he knows us."

"I heard some freaky stuff about the singer." Ryder moves behind Olivia. We're dancing exactly as we did that first night. Except...

"No wig," I tell her, close to her ear so she'll hear me. "You aren't worried about the press?"

"My mom isn't hiding my relationship with you two, and I no longer care who knows," she says, beaming at me.

My heart gives a happy thump in my chest and I exchange a look with Ryder over Olivia's shoulder. He nods. Fuck yeah. Tonight's the night. I knew it would be.

I hold her waist while Ryder hold her hips and we slowly dance and grind to the Bastian Crown song. The slow, sultry beat is audible sex. I kiss Olivia, thrusting my tongue into her mouth. She gasps against my lips, and I look down to see Ryder's hand creeping beneath her dress. I know the sweetness of her center, the gush of her arousal, the way she gets off when she's being watched or doing something risky. I kiss down her moans as Ryder plays with her pussy, and then I put my hand around her neck, holding her throat and making sure she's watching me when she comes.

"I like eye contact, Babydoll, remember?" I ask.

She nods and cries out. Her sounds of bliss are obscured by the volume of the music, her body hidden from anyone else's view by both Ryder and me wrapped around her like this. She's ours and ours alone.

I give her another kiss, then pull back and spin her around so she's facing Ryder. He licks his fingers, watching her face while he does it, and then he kisses her, too.

A satisfied grin on his face, he looks at me and nods.

It's time to go upstairs.

Olivia

My heart is so full, my body so alive. I just had an amazing orgasm at the hands of the two men I love while dancing in a crowded club, and I am one hundred percent happy. Their hands return to my hips and waist, and they're so warm through my dress, it's as if I'm naked to their touch.

"Upstairs, Babydoll," Jaxon says in my ear. "Now."

"Upstairs?" I ask, my legs shaking from the intense orgasm.

"Are you questioning our authority?" Ryder asks, a sadistic gleam in his blue eyes.

"No, Daddy," I say, moving toward the stairway. I've never been back this way before, but I trust my daddies.

They walk behind me, and I know without turning around that they're staring at my ass as I go up the stairs. I put an extra sway in my gait, feeling slickness between my thighs with every step.

"We have a private room tonight," Ryder says, catching up with me and taking my hand in his.

He leads me to a hall, and then a door, which he unlocks with a key card. The three of us step inside, and the pounding bass from the music softens to a dull thump. Enough to give us the flavor of the music without assaulting our ears or making conversation difficult.

The room is beautiful, done up in all black with creamy highlights. A set of loveseats crowd around a low table where a bottle of champagne rests in a bucket, with three glasses waiting next to it. A large painting depicts cream roses in a black vase and takes up the rear wall. The front of the room is all windows and looks out over the dance floor. We even have a little balcony so we can go out and dance without being crushed by a hundred other people.

"Do you like it?" Ryder asks.

I clap my hands together. "This room is amazing! I never noticed these spaces up here."

"Most people don't think to look up," Jaxon says with a smile.

I throw myself onto one of the love seats, then jump up and move to the door that opens to the balcony. "Can I go look?"

"Of course, Babydoll," Jaxon says, so I hurry over and pull open the door.

Music washes over me again, loud as before, and I lean slightly over the balcony so I can get a good view of the dancers. Ryder and Jaxon come to stand on either side of me.

A familiar man moves in the crush of bodies, dancing with a blond woman.

"Is that...is that Terrence, down there?" I ask, pointing.

Jaxon glances down and nods. "Yep, looks like."

I want to watch Terrence dance, because it's so strange to see him letting loose. I've only ever seen him working and he's always so stoic. Now, he still looks stoic, but there's a happy freedom in the way he moves his body. He's still favoring his left leg, but I'm thrilled to see that he's well enough to dance on it.

"Want some champagne, Olivia?" Jaxon asks me.

"Yeah," I say.

He holds out his hand, and I take it to follow him back into the room. Ryder comes with us, closing the door and once again dulling the noise of the music.

"This is so special, you guys," I say. "Thank you for arranging this evening."

"We want it to be special for you," Ryder says, kissing my cheek. "We want this night to be perfect."

There's a strange new tone in his voice, and I look at him curiously.

"Olivia," Jaxon says, taking one of my hands.

Ryder takes my other hand.

In one smooth motion, they both take a knee.

My two commanding, dominant men are both on their knees in front of me, their gazes hopeful as they stare at my face.

All of a sudden, I realize what's happening. At least, I think I know what's happening. My heart pounds rapid-fire in my chest, louder than the bass had been when we danced down in the club.

"Daddies?" I say, uncertain. I could be reading this wrong, and then I'll be crushed, and then...

"Olivia. Babydoll," Jaxon says, "breathe, sweetheart."

I take a deep breath.

"Good girl," he says, smiling. He continues, "You have been the absolute joy of my life ever since I laid eyes on you. If you agree to marry me, I'll be one of the two happiest men on the planet."

Before I can say anything, Ryder speaks. "Olivia, I was drawn to you from the beginning, although my own hang-ups caused me to miss out on your love initially..."

"You had my love," I whisper. "From the start, you had it. You both did."

"I didn't deserve it," he says. "But I'm so grateful you gave it to me, then, and now. I love you so fucking fiercely, it will make me one of the two happiest men on Earth if you'll agree to be my wife."

They each let go of my hands and reach into their pockets before pulling out tiny velvet boxes.

Pleasurable chills erupt over my arms and along my back. This moment is utterly, absolutely perfect, and I love them so damn much, my heart feels like it will burst with happiness.

"Will you marry us?" they ask in unison, opening the boxes. Matching rings sparkle up at me from each box, narrow bands with twin diamonds that I can already see are meant to be worn together.

Tears spill from my eyes and I make a sound between laughter and a sob. "Yes! Yes, I'll marry you both."

Their faces break out in huge smiles and they stand up, pulling me into a hug between them. I'm squeezed tightly, enveloped by their love. I smell Jaxon's citrus and leather, Ryder's pine forest. I'm home—this is home, this is love. These two men. They're mine.

They let me go and Jaxon puts his engagement ring on my finger before taking my mouth in a kiss that has my pussy getting even wetter than it had been. Ryder takes his turn next, his full lips nipping at mine while he fits the ring into place.

Jaxon opens the bottle of champagne and pours three glasses. We clink them together and I'm crying and laughing at the same time, gasping for enough breath so that I can take a sip of the drink and celebrate this insanely perfect moment.

"I'm so happy," I say, looking at Jaxon and Ryder. "So freaking happy."

Ryder grins and kisses my ring finger. "I doubt you're as happy as me, Babydoll."

"Or me," Jaxon says, wrapping an arm around my waist.

It's an argument none of us will ever win, and that's fine with me. I kiss Jaxon's cheek. "I want to dance some more, but I don't want to go downstairs with everyone else."

"That's what the balcony's for, sweetheart," he says.

We take our champagne to the balcony and sway to the music. Their hands skim over my body as we move, seemingly absentminded touches that only serve to stoke my desire. These are probably calculated moves by the men, because I doubt anything they do with me is thoughtless. But when I look at either of their faces to see if their expressions betray their intentions, I get no clue as to what their plans are.

The champagne makes me feel bold, and I lean against Jaxon's arm, pressing my breast against his bicep.

"I want you, Daddy. I want both of you."

"Greedy little girl," he says, amusement in his voice. "Didn't you just get an orgasm a few minutes ago?"

I turn to Ryder and say, "I want more, please, Daddy."

He grins and kisses my cheek. "Then more you shall have. Hold still."

He drops to his knees and lifts the bottom of my dress.

"Daddy, what are you doing?" I ask, looking down.

"Eyes on me, Babydoll," Jaxon says, tilting my chin until I face him.

Ryder's lips travel over my left thigh, then my right, and then he's back to my center and he starts lapping at my pussy and I'm gasping. I have to grip the edge of the balcony to keep from toppling over.

Jaxon holds my hips, adding some stability. And holding my dress up, out of Ryder's way. Jaxon nuzzles my neck, just beneath my ear. I love the feeling of his beard against my skin. I reach back and slide my hand over the hard length of his cock, feeling how hot and thick he is. I want him so badly, and Ryder, too.

"Maybe we should go home," I say.

"But you're all dressed up, Babydoll," Jaxon says. "We can't go back so soon."

"But I want to fuck," I whisper.

"We don't need to go home for that," he says, biting the edge of my ear.

I'm so wet, my arousal is dripping down my thighs. It won't take much to get me coming again. Maybe just a finger. If Ryder would just add a finger, I'd be exploding in seconds.

But instead of doing what I desperately need him to do, Ryder stands up.

"No, go back," I say, trying to push his shoulders down.

He just laughs and wipes his mouth on the back of his hand before leaning in to kiss me.

"I'm going to fuck your delicious pussy now, princess. Jax is going to take your ass. We'll have you coming again in this club tonight. Are you ready?"

"Yes." I nod to emphasize my answer. "Yes, I'm ready."

Ryder's gaze is hot on mine as he unfastens his pants just enough to pull his cock free. I want to drop to my knees and suck him—he looks delicious and lickable as a lollipop—but I'm so desperate to have my men inside my body, I try to be patient as he steps forward. He bends his knees and pulls one of my legs around his waist, spreading me for his intrusion.

"You ready, Babydoll?"

"I'm ready, Daddy."

He kisses my lips and thrusts up into me at the same time.

Pure delight.

I tremble in his arms. His cock is so large, I want to start moving, flexing my muscles and working to ease the fullness.

"Hold still, princess," Ryder whispers, kissing my

neck, my cheek, my lips. "We'll start moving in a minute. Be patient."

Behind me, Jaxon pulls a small bottle from his pocket.

"You brought lube?" I ask, even though: of course he did. They probably planned this. They've probably been planning this night for over a week.

He doesn't answer. Instead, he slicks some of it over his cock and leaves some on his fingers to press against my sensitive back hole. "You're going to take me here, Babydoll."

"Yes, Daddy," I say.

A second later, the wide head of his cock is pressing against my back entrance.

"Let me in," he growls.

I push out and he murmurs a nonsense sound of approval as he slides past the tight ring of muscle.

"So good, Babydoll," he whispers. "So fucking good."

And it *is* so fucking good. Ryder and Jaxon move slowly, working me up, sliding along sensitive nerve endings, lighting my body up with pleasure. I wrap one arm around Ryder's shoulders and use the other to grab Jaxon's leg, pulling him against me.

The music of the club surrounds us, muffling the sounds of our bodies moving together as the men thrust. Every movement ratchets my pleasure higher, heating me from my core outward. Every movement is delightful torture. I never want it to stop, but I fear the end.

"Such a sweet little girl," Jaxon says in my ear. "You're ours, Babydoll."

"Always ours," Ryder adds. "Even when we're fucking you in public."

I follow his gaze to the club below. The balcony wall

reaches almost to my chest. Nobody downstairs will be able to see a thing. If someone looks up, will they suspect?

Probably. It's too dark to see our faces or any defining details up here, but our shapes might be visible.

Do I care?

I'm too far gone in pleasure to care. Nothing is more important than the violent ecstasy ripping through my system.

"Come for your daddies," Ryder whispers, pressing his forehead to mine and looking into my eyes.

The feelings of bliss and pleasure are too much for my body to contain. They burst outward. My limbs tighten, my pussy rhythmically pulses, my breathing stops for a moment in a gasp.

"Daddy, Daddy," I cry.

They are everything—my world starts and ends with them.

Ryder makes a strangled sound and kisses me, his cock pulsing in my pussy as he comes. Jaxon bites my shoulder—I freaking love it when he does that—and empties into me as well.

We separate, not saying anything. Words aren't enough for what we mean to each other. But each man takes my hand, the one where my engagement rings sparkle and intertwine with each other, and they each give it a sweet, reverent kiss.

We belong to each other. They've claimed me.

I'm thoroughly possessed. Thoroughly theirs. Always their Babydoll.

∾

THANK you for reading *Their Babydoll*! I truly hope you enjoyed it.

If you want more of Olivia, Jaxon, and Ryder, you can visit https://calistajayne.com/their-babydoll-bonus/ to grab a bonus scene that takes place after their honeymoon. I promise, it isn't necessary for your enjoyment or full comprehension of their story—it is a true bonus scene. And yes, I am luring you in to sign up for my newsletter, but I'm not your boss or your Dom, so if you don't want the newsletter later, you can always unsubscribe!

The next series I wrote is *Cinderella's Daddies*, and you can find the first book, *Falling for Them*, on all major retailers. Visit https://calistajayne.com/cinderellas-daddies/ for links and info.

ALSO BY CALISTA JAYNE

Their Rebellious Princess

Their Rebellious Princess

Their Naughty Princess

Their Ruined Princess

Their Beloved Princess

My Vampire Doms

Ouch! My Vampire Doms Keep Biting Me

Ouch! My Vampire Doms Don't Sparkle

Ouch! My Vampire Doms Built a Scary Dungeon

Ouch! My Vampire Doms Have Really Long...Fangs

Ouch! My Vampire Doms Give Good Spankings

Ouch! My Vampire Doms Stole My Heart

Their Little Liar

Filthy Fiction

Dirty Diction

Tempting Tales

Naughty Novels

Their Babydoll

Daddies' Girl

Daddies' Babydoll

Daddies' Little Angel

Daddies' Princess

Daddies' Sweetheart

Daddies Ever After

Cinderella's Daddies

Falling for Them

Kneeling for Them

Submitting to Them

Belonging to Them

Fiercely Filthy Fairy Tales

Little Red's Temptation

Rapunzel's Sweet Release

Babydolls Standalones

Playing by Their Rules

Daddies' Little Troublemaker

ACKNOWLEDGMENTS

First, my thanks goes to you, dear reader! I am humbled and gratified that you started this series and read the entire sexy saga. I really hope you enjoyed it!

Many thanks, as always, goes to the Babydolls Club. You make this process so delightful! A special shout-out goes to our Sweethearts: Sarah Kruger-Padgett, Athena Marie, Jamie G, Kylilah, Elizabeth P, Siobhanmom40, Tina B, and Claudia. I appreciate your support more than words can express.

ABOUT THE AUTHOR

Calista Jayne adores filthy, smutty romances featuring dominant-yet-tender men. When not writing or reading, she's falling in love with the heroes in K-dramas or walking along a California beach.

Join Calista's newsletter to get showered in love notes (also known as newsletters and updates about new releases and sales) and receive a free book. Visit https://calistajayne.com/babydolls-newsletter to sign up!

Better yet, you can pamper yourself like the princess you are by joining Calista's Babydolls Club. Find everything you need to know here: https://calistajayne.com/club

Milton Keynes UK
Ingram Content Group UK Ltd.
UKHW051326260524
443099UK00004B/182

9 798224 016464